CADE

ALEXANDER SHIFTER BROTHERS
BOOK TWO

SELINA COFFEY

LOVY BOOKS

Jacqui

Miami Beach, Florida
Twenty Five Years Ago

*L*ess than four years old, Jacqui hid behind the couch as her parents argued. Lately, strange things had been happening, people were coming in and taking things from the house and her mommy had stopped buying her whatever she pointed at. Daddy had started to yell at her mommy too. She didn't like Daddy yelling at Mommy.

Jacqui's long blonde hair, fine and silky, was tied at the nape of her neck but she wished she could let it down. She liked to hide behind it when she couldn't escape her parents arguing. Mommy got mad when she let it down so she left it alone, hoping her hands over her ears would block out the arguing.

"Why can't you unbind her powers? You're a witch for crying out loud, you can do anything!" Jacqui's father screamed at her mother, his eyes bulging and desperate.

"I told you it can't be undone until she marries. You knew better, you wouldn't listen! Besides, you've all but used up my powers and now we're out of luck. And magic!" Jacqui's mother, a mirror image of her beautiful daughter, looked different tonight. Her normally serene, unlined features looked older, harsher somehow.

"Well, something has to be done. It's all gone, all the money is gone!"

"That's not my fault, Edmund! I told you not to go into cocaine! We had enough money but oh no, you were too greedy to turn down an opportunity. Now look where we're at. You're lucky you didn't wind up in prison. Imagine, Tanya Evans brought down to a mobile home in a trailer park! It wasn't this bad when I was a stripper! We don't even have power now, the company pulled the meter off the wall! This is the "everything" you promised me huh, Edmund?"

Jacqui didn't know what all of the words meant but she knew her parents weren't happy anymore. Ever since the policeman took Daddy away that day over a year ago, things had gone downhill. When Daddy came back things had changed, her mother had become a woman of anger and tears, instead of the smiles and love she used to shower on her daughter. Jacqui had come to accept, over time, that Mommy and Daddy had changed but she didn't know why. She couldn't figure out what she'd done wrong. She decided it was better to take a nap, maybe things would be quiet after a nap, they sometimes were.

The fight raged on and Jacqui woke up a few times, screams piercing her dreams, screams of anger, of pain. Shattering glass woke her at one point but she simply rolled over, not wanting to look, to see what had happened. She just wanted to live in a world of quiet, with no shouting, where she had enough to eat and her dolls back. Maybe a puppy would be nice. With her tiny thumb between her lips, Jacqui settled back into sleep.

THE MONTHS PASSED and Daddy started to act strange, slurring his words and falling over a lot. Mommy yelled at him about getting a job but he'd just keep drinking from his special glass, the one Jacqui wasn't allowed to touch. When Daddy left one night and didn't come back, Jacqui's mommy started leaving at night, locking her softly crying daughter in her bedroom as she went out in skimpy clothes.

Jacqui heard the other women in the trailer park talking and learned her mommy was a stripper. She didn't know what *that meant but she knew it mustn't be anything good by the way the women sneered the word.*

Years passed and Jacqui became a young woman. She'd found out at sixteen that her father killed himself when she was six, jumping off a bridge into the ocean, never to be seen again. Life hadn't improved for young Jacqui. Her mother was a drug addict now and Jacqui had to hide the money she made from her after-school job at a local restaurant. She worked hard, made good grades, but she had no plans to go to college, there just wasn't money for it and her mom needed her.

Jacqui loved her mother but the years of hardship and neglect had taken their toll. When you knew almost every STD, drug, and "trick" men expected from their prostitute by the time you were eighteen, your relationship with your mother was strained, to say the least. Jacqui's mother stole from her own daughter to buy the drugs she craved and Jacqui paid the price, going hungry until she earned the money back at her job.

Jacqui wasn't sure if she felt despair or grief more when her mother died. She just knew she felt numb. Numb but free. She also felt a lot of guilt; she hadn't been enough to save her mother. That was a heavy burden for an eighteen-year-old girl to carry around with her.

Instead of going to her graduation ceremony, Jacqui attended her mother's funeral. There she met an elderly woman who changed her life. The woman was beautiful, even with a lined face and a rounded back. Time had stooped the woman but her fire and will had not waned.

Evelyn Sawyers saved Jacqui from the same fate as her mother. She told Jacqui of how she'd saved Tanya from a life of stripping and set her up with a fantastic life, she'd just let her heart rule her instead of her head. Evelyn taught Jacqui all she knew about men, about how to please them in every imaginable way, and about how to wrap them around her fingers.

Jacqui had been appalled at first, her mother had been a dirty prostitute, a drug addicted hag at the end, she didn't want the same life. Evelyn told Jacqui about her mother meeting a waiter at a restaurant one night and falling in love. Love had ruined Tanya. Jacqui swore she wasn't going to make the same mistake her mother made. She'd never love a man, not the way Tanya had loved Edmund.

She escorted very rich men to parties, but she never slept with any of them. Known by many in her world as an ice-queen, Jacqui could have made far more money if she'd given up her virginity but she wouldn't allow herself to take that step. It might invite emotion in and she could not allow herself to lose any control. She didn't want to end up like her mother.

She made a lot of money in her eleven years with Evelyn, despite not sleeping with the clients. Now she was looking for a new life. A life of a similar quiet atmosphere and peace. She wanted to live in peace. That was all she wanted. Maybe a

*puppy too. She still hadn't got that puppy she'd always
wanted.*

* * *

Miami, Florida
Present

JACQUI PUT down her smartphone and looked out at the
people buzzing past the street café she was sitting at.
Well-dressed tourists walked by, trying to look as
though they belonged by not gawking at everything that
looked exceptionally expensive, amusing Jacqui. They
were almost harder to take seriously than the ones
dressed in the cheap bikinis and flip-flops from the
discount stores that dotted parts of Florida. Snobbery
for snobbery's sake always amused Jacqui.

She came from humble beginnings and though she
was now rich, she felt like she didn't quite fit in. She hid
those feelings behind ice-blue eyes and pale skin, far
paler than anyone living in Florida had a right to be, but
she managed to protect herself from the sun's harsh rays
with her clothes and a lot of careful planning. Along
with gallons of sunblock.

Just now she was sitting beneath an umbrella, her
eyes protected by large designer sunglasses, watching

6

the tourists go by. Sometimes she came down from her high-rise world, down to the ground, just to make sure it still existed. The only time she left otherwise was to go somewhere with a client. Her needs were cared for by a wealthy patron, a man that had his own proclivities but kept Jacqui around for appearance's sake. Just one of many men she'd served over her life as an escort.

She was a front, a haven, a ruse for gay men that refused to be dragged out of the closet. She was paid well for her services but sometimes she needed to come back down to the real world. Jacqui shifted as she spotted the woman she was meeting and held her arm out. The woman saw her and came to sit with Jacqui.

"Good morning my darling, how are you?" Carla held her hand out to Jacqui, her own eyes hidden behind large glasses but her beautifully full lips stretched in a warm smile.

"I'm fine, Carla, want a drink?" Jacqui took the other woman's hand and squeezed before she let it go. Besides Evelyn, this was the only other soul on earth that Jacqui had formed any kind of bond with. As Evelyn's personal assistant, Carla knew about Jacqui's life but did not intrude on it or judge her, she simply acted as a friend to the other woman. When Jacqui allowed it.

Tall, Latin and beautiful, Carla was a dream come true for many but she had no time for such things. Her life as a child had not been so great either and she was also one of Evelyn's foundlings. Carla had chosen a different path in her life than Jacqui but she was still well-cared for.

"Have you considered Liam's offer?" Jacqui's eyes narrowed as she looked at her friend, watching for any clue Carla might give away. Carla was a professional ice queen too, she had to be in her line of work, and gave nothing away. Jacqui knew a man had recently offered quite a bit of money for a night with Carla but Carla had refused to answer so far.

"I have. I'm considering it. But for now, I'm here to talk about you. Here is the list you requested." Carla slid a folder over to Jacqui and Jacqui took it.

Pictures of very handsome men with their profiles outlined filled the folder, an inch thick. This was another of Evelyn's services, men who required wives but didn't want questions asked. They wanted a woman with an impeccable past with excellent skills at hiding the truth. The need for secrecy was obvious when she saw that many were politicians and men with a need to hide their sexuality. The world had become more accepting of homosexuality, but for those in the higher echelons of power, the need to hide their true selves seemed to be necessary. Others were in fields ruled by men that would see a gay male as weak.

Others, such as a few of the actors Jacqui now saw in the folder, had contracts with their studios that held a clause that they would not disclose their sexuality. Straight women wanted straight male heartthrobs, not gay men that were completely unattainable. The illusion that there might be a chance, some windswept night when the stars aligned, had to be there and gay actors didn't often get leading male roles.

Jacqui suppressed the urge to raise her eyebrows at some of the names she found in the folder. She'd have never guessed about the men she recognized. She'd simply had no clue.

"Shocking isn't it?" Carla sipped at a mojito as Jacqui flipped pages.

"It is. Sometimes I feel like my entire life has been an illusion." She sighed and put the folder down. She'd have to make a choice within 24 hours then incinerate the folder. Secrecy must be maintained.

"That's why we do what we do, Jacqui. I'm glad to see you're going for some kind of normal, though. Even if the marriage is a sham."

"This life can be a long one. Eleven years feels like a hundred, you know?" Jacqui brushed a sleek lock behind her ear and began to eat the salad the waiter brought out to her.

"I understand. Evelyn says to let her know your

choice and she'll send another envelope over with the details." In an age where electronics could be hacked, paper could still burn. Most of the information about clients was kept out of computer systems and could be incinerated at a moment's notice.

"I'll let her know." Jacqui's naturally strong white teeth picked a black olive from her fork delicately, seductively, without any effort. She was trained to give an illusion and though she'd never been with a man she'd made many quiver just by eating in front of them. The skills had become second nature to her now and she didn't even notice Carla watching her avidly.

"I'll miss you, you know." Carla's words were an admission that would normally not have been spoken and Jacqui looked up at her friend.

They were friends but a lot had remained unsaid between them, neither wanting to fall into the world of even platonic love. Emotion was an enemy and to be squashed. But something was different about Carla today and for a moment Jacqui's façade cracked.

"Will you?" Curiosity weighted her words and Jacqui looked away, hoping her sunglasses still hid her eyes the way Carla's hid her dark chocolate brown ones.

"Yes, I will. But that's to be expected. So, I've decided to accept the offer. It happens in two days. Maybe I'll use some of the money to come visit you wherever you end up." Carla knew Jacqui would never accept anyone in Miami so travel would have to be involved.

Jacqui felt a prickle of annoyance. She'd have to hide her past in her new life, Carla would not only be a reminder of that past, she'd be a clue. But the annoyance was subsumed by a quiver of delight. Jacqui suspected Carla was infatuated with her but neither had ever broached the subject. Maybe that's what drove Carla to take the offer and make the admission.

Jacqui had noted the sideways glances over the years, the lingering touches, but had never allowed herself to consider taking the friendship further. She'd felt curiosity the same as she had with men, she just wouldn't allow herself to be weak. Sex made you weak. Even with women.

"That would be lovely." Jacqui let the words break through, her long years of friendship with the woman finally winning out. She couldn't look at Carla after she said the words so she went back to staring at the people passing by, her salad forgotten.

"That's settled then. I have to get back to the office. Message me later with your decision." Carla bent to give Jacqui's cheek an air kiss before she walked way, quickly disappearing into the crowds.

Inhaling deeply, Jacqui left some money with the waiter and left. She had to make a decision quickly. She assumed any man would do what she wanted. A sexless life as a decoration when needed, a woman that could pursue her own interests otherwise. A life of no children, with a husband that led a quiet life. She'd already dismissed the politicians and military men. Too much spotlight was placed on those type of men, she wanted a quiet man with no aspirations in politics or fame. If the man was well-known that was fine, but she didn't want someone the press would hound for all their days.

Back at her crisp, white, minimalist apartment, Jacqui settled down onto a red velvet couch, her bare feet tucked beneath her. One man had piqued her interest and she went back to him. Cade Alexander was tall, dark, and at thirty-six years of age, he was very handsome. There was something cold about him though, something in his black eyes that seemed to push people away, even from a photograph. His sexuality was not listed but she had to assume he was just as homosexual as the others.

A rancher in Kansas, Cade was looking for a woman of her age, with her looks, and for the same reasons, she wanted a husband. A quiet, sexless, childless marriage so he could focus on his own life while letting the world think he was married and happy.

He was perfect really, not so old she'd be called a gold-digger behind her back, and not too young. He wasn't ostentatious or dramatic looking, he was just a rancher in a suit. A very handsome rancher. Jacqui reminded herself she wasn't looking for love and took his picture out of the file. This was the one.

She'd start an email exchange with him this evening and hopefully, arrangements would soon be made. As the wife of a rancher, she'd be left in peace, with a secure future. And if something happened, well, she had her own nest egg to fall back on. This marriage idea appealed because she'd be able to have more security but if it did not work out then it was alright.

Jacqui knew she wasn't leading the normal life and never would. She wanted the illusion of it though, for her own security. Only in her dreams at night did she long for love, to be touched, that was the one arena of her life she couldn't control. She took pains to become adept at forgetting her dreams as time went by, now she barely knew if she dreamed at all.

She'd worked to leave her past behind, to build a façade around herself that was next to impossible to crack. She hadn't cried since the day her mother died. She could laugh, but to feel genuine love, care or heart-break was not something she was willing to ever experience again. Jacqui wasn't a cruel person, she was just unyielding and determined to never feel what she'd felt her entire childhood ever again.

Love made you weak, vulnerable and a target. Jacqui knew she never wanted to experience any of that ever again. Her father had left her, her mother had left her, and she'd had no one else to turn to. Nobody but Evelyn, and from her Jacqui learned to make it in this world. She hadn't wanted fame or notoriety, she just wanted security. Evelyn had given that to her and Jacqui knew that Cade would do the same by offering her the same as she offered him, an illusion for the world.

2

Jacqui

Jacqui heard her phone vibrating and picked it up, her heart tripping for a moment. It was Cade. He'd responded to her email quickly and with interest. That was a good sign.

Jacqui wasn't certain why her heart tripped but she squashed the excitement. This was a business transaction like any other, she told herself, no need to go acting like a besotted teenager. No reason at all.

She opened the email and found a cordial response, an introductory note more than anything.

"Hello, may I have your file please?"

Jacqui sent the file as requested, and waited. The file

contained all of her information, her past, her present, everything from her bank account information to her underwear sizes. Birthdate, parentage, any notable events that might make for tabloid fodder. Evelyn prided herself on running a business with the future of her clients in mind; no hidden secrets would tarnish the reputation of her clients from her girls.

Her phone chirped again and she opened the email.

"I'll get back to you within twenty-four hours. Good evening."

Jacqui raised her left eyebrow and looked down at the phone with detachment.

He was very formal but this was only their introduction. Besides, wasn't this what she wanted, only the illusion of matrimony without the caring and emotions part to make it all mucky?

Jacqui put her phone down and pulled herself from the hot embrace of the bathtub, reaching for a plush towel to dry herself. Cade was exactly what she wanted and she knew she could have him. She was perfect, if you put a spin on the events from her childhood. She'd overcome all obstacles to emerge humble but successful in her life, a butterfly forged from an iron cocoon.

Opening a bottle of wine, she sat down to read through Cade's file once more. A man of simple, if boring tastes. He'd rarely gone abroad, did not like nightclubs or parties, and spent most of his days working, in meetings, or asleep. His interests included wood carving and book restoration. That must be old books, antiques or something. She imagined that could bring many interesting books to his doorstep. He also liked to knit. Knitting?

"How incredibly dreary," Jacqui muttered to herself, the quiet inside of her apartment almost too much for a moment.

She'd wanted it all as a child; the husband, family, the white picket fence. But now she just wanted to live with as little drama as possible. Her father had been a very rich man once, with a collection of cars and houses, but that had all gone away. Then he'd gone away, emotionally at first, physically next. Then her mother had done the same. She'd had a lifetime of excitement and adventure before she'd even turned 18. Now she just wanted to make it through without another day of drama.

A new email set her phone to buzzing and she opened it.

"Do you agree to the conditions?"

Concise, to the point, and expecting an answer. This was an alpha male for all his knitting and bookbinding. His emails disclosed a man used to being answered, not answering questions, and a man used to giving orders. Jacqui gleaned that from their few exchanges. There was no reason for pretense in this matter so she knew this was how the man was used to addressing people.

"I agree, do you agree to mine?" She sent the email quickly, wanting to ensure he'd read through her file properly.

"I'll get back to you."

"Oh indeed, you'll get back to me. Take your time but don't wait too long or this butterfly will fly away." She returned to leafing through his file.

He had several brothers and both of his parents were deceased. There'd been a recent addition to the family when his brother married and the new wife was expecting a child. There was the heir to the throne, at least. Jacqui knew she was being cynical but that is how she approached life now, with sense and logic.

She read his non-disclosure agreement, the prenuptial agreement, and the clauses that would make all void. There were the usual instances of no open adultery, clauses regarding illegitimate children she may produce from the expected well-hidden affairs and how he would accept them as his own, and the absolute hard limits on the use of drugs. There were quite a few clauses about secrecy as well.

Jacqui assumed those clauses regarded his homosexuality and keeping it hidden. She had no problem with hiding secrets, but this seemed to imply there might be something more. Familial secrets, what did that mean exactly? Apparently, this would not be disclosed until sometime after the wedding. Smart man, wives didn't have to testify against husbands. Now why did she think of that, she wondered.

Flicking a well-manicured nail against her teeth, Jacqui wondered what other secrets Mr. Alexander was hiding. This part of Evelyn's service, the marriage brokering, usually took place over the phone, with emails, and through a fax machine. She wasn't going to have time to delve into pasts too deeply and honestly, she really didn't care. Jacqui knew that she'd likely not meet Cade until the day of their marriage and that was fine with her. They'd both have to play the part of the happy couple occasionally, but after the wedding they'd go back to being their own people, at least behind closed doors. She dismissed the niggling worry and put his file down.

Perhaps she should look at others, just in case. She was going through the file of a blond god in the soldier-adventure writing field when her phone buzzed again.

Jacqui's left eyebrow quirked. Meet? Highly unusual but not unheard of.

"Of course, send me the arrangements." He'd have to pay for it and arrange it all if he wanted to meet first, that's just how it was.

Just before she went to bed she received another email. This time, flight details and boarding passes came through. She was heading to Kansas in less than 24 hours on a chartered flight. That should prove interesting.

Sure of herself and of her abilities to please a man, even if it wasn't sexually, Jacqui went to bed prioritizing things she needed to do before her trip. It would be hectic but she could get it all done. That's why he was going to marry her, after all, her efficiency if nothing else.

* * *

THE BLACK CAR that collected Jacqui from the airport pulled into the driveway and Jacqui stared at the house, a beautiful creation of local materials and stone. She tapped at her lower teeth in irritation. She'd received a text from Cade as soon as she landed, advising her he'd be unable to pick her up, a family emergency required his attention.

Jacqui stepped out once the driver opened the door, her gray pantsuit still neat and tidy, as she ascended the steps. A careful woman, Jacqui rarely looked scruffy or out of place in most social situations. Her black heels, sexy but still sensible, clicked on the stone steps as she walked up to the door. A scream from inside stopped as soon as the doorbell rang.

Jacqui's left eyebrow went up in curiosity but little else showed her emotion. A young man, not much older than herself, opened the door, a frantic look on his face.

"You aren't the doctor! Where is the fu…" His words were cut off by a bellow from an unseen man.

"Kane, who's at the door? Is that the doctor? Don't just stand there you idiot, get over here, she's crowning!" The voice was similar to the man named Kane's voice, but deeper, smoother. There was also a note of panic.

"Crowning? Is there a coronation going on?" Jacqui asked the air because Kane quickly disappeared, running into a room off to the side of the entry. Jacqui followed, her curiosity definitely getting the better of her for a moment.

She'd had no idea life was about to turn upside down when she stepped on the plane this morning. No idea at all, she thought, as her eyes went round and she backed into the door that had somehow closed. A woman was there, a dark-skinned woman with no clothes on and her legs spread wide, something… Oh god.

Jacqui looked away quickly, trying to get the door to open but the knob simply refused to turn.

"Somebody, please. Let me out." Jacqui's words were quiet, her low voice smooth and rich. "Please."

None of the people in the room paid her any attention as the woman on the couch screamed, her wide ice-blue eyes so very startling. The woman's wail of exertion and pain petered out and the two men around her seemed to slump with her.

"Get that towel, Kane. The baby's almost out. A couple more pushes." The taller man, a photocopy of Kane with the exception of a few lines, reached for the towel and slid it under the emerging mass of hair and flesh coming from the woman's womb.

Jacqui wanted to look away but she felt drawn to the scene. She'd never witnessed a birth, not even an animal birth, and hadn't planned on it, but this woman's baby seemed to have a different idea. Jacqui swallowed down something like revulsion, wondering how the human body could stretch so much, and continued to watch as the woman tensed once more, all but sitting up against the armrest of a very expensive looking couch as she screamed out her effort.

The woman had delicate features but a strong jaw and teeth, and when her eyes popped open, boring into Jacqui, something happened. Something inside of Jacqui shifted, popped almost, and she knew this woman would be important throughout her life. Jacqui all but held her breath as the men at her feet started to grow tense, shifting their positions as a small bundle with black hair slithered from the woman.

She didn't think her eyes could go any wider but they did, and Jacqui felt something odd happening, something very distressing that she hadn't felt in a very long time. Her eyes were welling with tears! She wanted to hide, to get herself under control, but her feet were rooted until the baby's first cry of life. Then she stepped forward. Just a step, then another before she stopped.

There was nothing she could do to help, the quick efficient moves of the man beside Kane seemed to be all that was needed and soon he had the cord cut and the baby was laying on her mother's chest as the man did a few more things. Jacqui had eyes only for the baby and the mother as the men paced back and forth, doing things Jacqui wasn't aware of.

The mother's face was unlike anything Jacqui had ever seen on a person before. She wondered if her own mother had worn such a look on the day she was born. Jacqui's coldness thawed for a moment and she had to fight back a sob of joy. She'd just seen life come into the world!

The woman wiped at the baby with a towel as the man, the child's father from the look of awe on his own face, gave her washcloths from a clean bowl of hot water. The baby protested, waved her tiny fists, and scrunched up her tiny face, screaming her head off, until the mother gave the child her breast. That soon quietened the baby down.

Jacqui felt a smile tug at her lips and finally took a chair, unsure of what else to do. The woman had seen her, knew she was there, it might be rude to leave. How should one properly extricate themselves from a birth-crashing? Jacqui contemplated the matter as the woman was cleaned up, a bucket of towels and other things taken away, and a large towel was placed under her bottom. Jacqui heard the man taking the bucket out growling about the lazy doctor and how he was going to drill him a new one, and smiled.

She sat back in the seat, letting the new family have their moment as the man brought out a mop and bucket, then took it all away. If this was Cade he was very efficient, if very unobservant. He still hadn't noticed she was there.

Jacqui sat, quietly amused as she watched the man pacing back and forth with mops and blankets, baby clothes, and a diaper. He just kept going back and forth for at least 30 minutes before he settled down on the chair beside of her.

"I'm sorry, who are you?" His voice was strong, sure, and like smoke rolled into honey.

"I see that you're quite overwhelmed today. Perhaps

today wasn't the right time for me to come. I'm Jacqui Evans." I held my hand out to the man with a cool smile.

"OH! Oh my God! I am so, I must apologize!" The man stood, running his hands through hair that was short on the bottom but just slightly longer on top, giving him an almost boyish air. He looked around and looked as though he was about to explode when Jacqui stood with him and sat him back in the chair.

"I think you can be excused today, Cade. Helping to birth a child isn't an everyday occurrence after all. Shall I go and make some tea, prepare some drinks perhaps?"

He looked at her with gratitude and sat down in a chair while she prepared a drink for him and his brother. Jacqui found some juice and ice in a cabinet under the collection of bottles and made one for the woman as well. Handing them out from a silver tray she sat down, her own drink in hand.

"Now, when is this doctor arriving?" Jacqui had seen him angrily swiping his phone and assumed he was giving the doctor a piece of his mind.

"He should be here within the hour. It seems Damesha isn't the only one to give birth today." He all but growled the words but gave her a kinder look.

"Why haven't you taken her to a hospital? Or should I not ask?" She tapped at her bottom teeth with her nail again, wondering if she'd crossed a line.

"The nearest hospital is too far, it all went rather quickly and she didn't want to give birth there anyway. The doctor was supposed to come to supervise but as I said..." He gave her a look that said there wasn't anything more he could have done.

She supposed there wasn't much he could do, in that case. Deciding that quiet was best for now, she settled into a dark red chair of well-stained leather so red it was almost black, and waited for whatever was coming next.

She sat quietly, observing the house and the people inside of it. The couple were obviously delighted with the peacefully quiet baby and Cade sat stonily staring at his phone in between shooting glares at the door. She hid a smile, she'd been promised quiet and peace but had walked into the exact opposite.

Jacqui was used to a lack of conversation, generally her opinion wasn't wanted by the clients she served or the people they were around. She was little more than an ornament, really. Obviously, things were going to be the same in this situation too. That was fine, she was used to staying quiet, observing, and keeping things to herself. The practice had served her well so far.

The house was richly done, tasteful of course, but dark warm tones filled the room and the area she'd seen when she came in. There was very little in the way of color to shock the senses, all earth-tones and shades of white. Even the two men were dressed in dark shades, though Cade wore a dark gray dress shirt and black slacks while Kane wore black jeans and a black t-shirt. This was a family that liked nice things but kept a low profile. Good.

Jacqui stood when a man in a white lab-coat with a black bag walked into the room. Cade glared at him, promising to return shortly, and asked Jacqui to follow him. He led her to a door that took them outside. She was greeted with a large rectangular swimming pool surrounded with wood furniture and white umbrellas on the six tables. This house was obviously meant for more than one family member and was some kind of social center for the entire family. There weren't any other people out here and it was far quieter than in the house.

Cade led her to a table by a natural-looking but very small waterfall, and apologized.

"I'm sorry but I must speak with the doctor. I'll come back in a little while, if that's alright with you? I am deeply sorry about all of this." He looked contrite but distracted, almost boyish for a moment before he looked away.

"I understand, things do happen. I'll be fine out here, if someone can bring me a drink and maybe something to eat?" Jacqui looked at him with understanding.

"Thank you, of course, yes. I'll send someone out right away. It won't be a moment." He turned and walked away.

Jacqui watched him go and decided that he wasn't the stereotypical gay male. Definitely an alpha male, but polite and considerate, if somewhat formal and cold. This was their first meeting, though. She didn't hope for anything more than cordiality really, but perhaps a bit of warmth would be nice. Something had changed inside of her in the last hour, something she wasn't sure she entirely liked. That woman had done something to her, broken something inside of her, and this sudden need for warmth from a man she didn't even know was a bit embarrassing and distressing.

Jacqui told herself to shape up and asked for a drink and a sandwich from the young woman that appeared at her side. Jacqui hadn't seen her approach and startled when the woman spoke.

"I'll bring that right out." The woman left without introducing herself.

Jacqui felt a moment of disquiet. Was the woman staff or family? Either way, the entire household seemed to be uninterested in knowing who people were. That seemed odd to Jacqui but perhaps they were used to not asking questions. She felt an urge to tap at her teeth once more but squashed it, this was all proving strange.

A sandwich and her drink were brought out by a different young woman, and before Jacqui could try to speak to her the woman walked away. Shrugging at the whole thing, Jacqui began to eat her sandwich.

She jumped when something thumped against her back and she heard an odd noise from the back of the chair. Turning she saw a medium-sized dog that looked rather like a large beagle of red and white staring at her sandwich with longing. The dog turned brown eyes up at her with the saddest eyes she'd ever seen.

"Oh my. Where did you come from then?" Jacqui turned to pet the dog and saw a name on the collar. "Annie. Is that you?"

The dog grinned, gave a breathy sound of happiness, and shook her head. Well, Jacqui thought, that's a new one. A dog that answers you.

"Well, Annie, I have far too much sandwich here so would you like to share with me?"

Annie shook her head once more and did a little dance with her front paws. They were very large paws, much larger than she needed it seemed, but she knew how to use them. Jacqui smiled and fed the dog part of her roast beef sandwich. She was tickled when Annie very carefully took the bit of bread and meat from her fingers before wolfing it down greedily. Annie pranced again, waiting for more.

Jacqui fed more of the sandwich to the dog than to herself but she loved watching the way Annie delicately took each bite between her teeth, as though she were a very dignified lady, before letting instinct take over. Annie had a lot of self-control; that much was obvious.

Jacqui and Annie soon finished off the sandwich and waited for someone to come and retrieve them. Annie looked up at Jacqui happily as the woman scratched at her ears but started to get anxious. She kept going to the glass paneled door and then back to Jacqui. At first, she didn't make any noise but then a loud whining noise, almost a piercing whistle, started.

Jacqui didn't want to intrude on whatever was going on inside but when Annie started to jump up at the handle, as if she knew how to open it, Jacqui decided it was time to find somebody. The dog obviously belonged here and knew her way around. She wanted something so Jacqui let her in, following the dog as she sniffed at the air.

Annie seemed to have caught the scent she was looking for because her ears perked up and she took off for the room Jacqui had left an hour ago. There wasn't anyone in the room now but Annie had her nose to the floor, snuffling along as she followed a scent. Jacqui was fascinated with the dog and followed her up a curving set of stairs, up to a room with an open dark walnut door.

The couple in the room looked up at Jacqui as she came to the door. They looked confused at first, uncertain of why she was there probably, but then smiled when they saw Annie.

"Baby girl! Come meet your sister!" the woman called out to Annie, who had stopped at the door. The dog ran into the room and gingerly found a spot to sit where she could look up at the woman. "This is Elspeth, Annie. She's your sister."

The dog gently stuck her nose to the baby, sniffing the tiny girl, before barely sticking her tongue out to lick the back of the baby's head. The woman smiled down at Annie and they all settled together as the man came to Jacqui.

"I'm sorry, I don't know who you are but you must know Cade. Can I help you with anything? You're obviously waiting for something." His eyes were gentle, a dark to the woman's light, and he brought calm with him.

"Hi, my name's Jacqui. I have a meeting with your brother. I flew up from Florida this morning for it. Do you know where he is, perhaps?" She offered him a smile rather than her hand.

"Ah, right. He said he had an important meeting

today that we were fu…uh, right. No, I don't know where he is but he said something about dinner as he saw the doctor out. Obviously, we won't be coming down but I can show you where his office is." He gave her his own kind smile and Jacqui wondered if there was Native American in their ancestry.

Both men were dark, even their skin was a dark tan, and their eyes were unlike any brown she'd ever seen before. Kane was a gentler version of his brother and he offered to take her elbow as they walked back down the stairs. She politely refused, her heels weren't that high after all, and followed him.

"Congratulations by the way. You must be very excited." Jacqui felt awkward in the quiet as they walked and thought the baby might break the ice.

"Oh yes, she's our first. Thank you very much, and thank you for not panicking when you came in. Damesha wanted a quiet home birth but she wanted the doctor here. Baby Elspeth decided to come more quickly than we thought she would." He gave a grin of amusement and stopped in front of a door not far from the room they'd all been in earlier.

"This is his office. I'll be back off to see to Damesha if you don't mind. I hope your meeting goes well." With a twinkling gleam in his eyes and a quick smile, Kane dashed away, leaving her at the closed door.

She knocked softly, the way she'd been taught to, and went into the office when Cade's voice told her to come in.

"Oh, good grief, I left you outside, didn't I? What you must think of me! Do sit down." Jacqui noted he still hadn't spoken her name.

Jacqui took the leather chair opposite his desk and settled in. Maybe now they could have a discussion.

"Dinner will be served shortly. I hope you haven't changed your mind? Today was a bit, well, unusual." He looked down at his hands, his nails were neatly manicured and clean, his hands strong and capable.

Jacqui was certain the man was capable of handling his business affairs but the strength in those hands told her he wasn't afraid of hard work either.

"Do you help birth children often then? You seemed rather capable." She couldn't help her curiosity. Her control seemed to slip around him for some reason.

"I do with the sheep and cattle we raise on the ranch, but not with human children usually. I was flying by the seat of my pants and with skills I learned from a vet." He looked a bit bashful for a moment.

She could tell that he wasn't used to answering questions but seemed open to giving her that opportunity. Perhaps because she was soon going to be his wife? It wasn't that important that she knew anything about him more than what she'd already learned but it was nice to talk with him.

"Well, you did an admirable job. If you'll show me to my room, I'll change for dinner." She fell back on formality, the moment of warmth almost frightening her. This wasn't going how she'd planned at all.

"Of course. Follow me." He led her to a room on the bottom floor and she was soon changed and ready for dinner. A long sleeved black sweater along with a pair of black slacks were appropriate in the house. It was incredibly cold inside, even if it was warm outside of the walls and doors. She tied her hair in a knot on the back of her head and walked to the dining room Cade had shown her earlier.

They hadn't spoken much on the tour of the house, just a simple exchange about what each room was and how nice the house was. Jacqui would have found it all very boring but something about him made her feel warm inside. His scent filled her nose and she could feel him beside her, even with her eyes closed she could still feel Cade beside of her.

Maybe it was best if she went home? This awareness of him wasn't good for her, not good for her at all. Besides, he was gay! It wasn't like he'd be interested in her anyway. Maybe that was a good thing? Maybe she could let her guard down, if only a little, with him?

"Hello, Jacqui, thank you for joining me. It's just going to be us two this evening so I thought we'd eat outside by the pool, if you don't mind?" He'd been waiting for her in the dining room and stood as she came in. All formality back in place.

She gave a small nod in agreement and followed him.

"Now, I understand if you'd like to go back home after the events of today. Normally we are far more organized around here." He paused to pull her seat out for her. He sat in his own seat before speaking again. "I would like it if you'd give us another chance, however."

"Of course." She gave him a small smile before looking down at the food. She wanted to distract herself. Several times today she'd felt a warmth towards him, a thawing of her cold shell, but now the wall was back up. His formality came with cordiality but it brought her own walls back up.

"Thank you. Now, if you don't mind discussing things over dinner, I'd appreciate it. I have another meeting in an hour I need to be on time for." He didn't seem to notice that the words were just a bit rude or how Jacqui stiffened.

"Not at all." Her words were stilted and the beautiful dinner spread out before them seemed to lose its flavor as he spoke.

The duck seemed cold and oily, the vegetables wilted and limp as she listened to him.

"I'd like to have the wedding here, if you don't mind. You'll be given an account to get whatever you need and arrangements have been made with a wedding planner so you won't need to worry over that. I know this is a formal arrangement so I assumed you wouldn't be overly concerned with details. We'll leave it all up to the planner shall we?" He cut slices from his duck, eating just as delicately as Annie had earlier. He had beautiful table manners but it was back to business and that all but shut Jacqui's brain down.

"Of course, whatever you'd like." She let her walls grow just a little icier as she ate her dinner. This was what she'd chosen, after all.

This is why she didn't allow herself to be weak, those moments this afternoon made the whole dinner incredibly painful. With her walls in place, the pain soon disappeared.

The dessert, a rather grand tiramisu when it first appeared, seemed soggy and tasteless when she started to eat it. She wouldn't make the same mistake twice. From now on she was the ice queen, no matter how tempting Cade Alexander might be.

3

Cade

A week later, Cade lounged in a hot tub, preparing for another dinner with Jacqui that evening. His family was shocked about the woman's role in his life, of course, but knew better than to question his decision. He and Jacqui had prepared a story about meeting a few months earlier when he'd visited Florida. None of his family would question the falsehood, Cade was the head of the family, head of the clan, and his word was law.

He'd thought a long time before seeking out a mail-order bride. The term was old-fashioned, he knew, but that's what she was, really. He'd put in a request with a business he knew of and they'd sent him an ice-queen, just what he'd ordered. She'd seemed to thaw a few times but her shields had gone right back up.

He'd liked how she responded to the chaos of the afternoon, how she'd dealt with the aftermath and his callousness. She'd passed the test, she'd do. It didn't hurt that she was beautiful, tempting, and lovely. It didn't help either, however. Kane had produced an heir, that's all the clan needed. They'd wanted Cade to marry, harassing him with offers for daughters he'd known his whole life, women just like himself. He didn't want that, he didn't want a mate, he didn't want a soul-mate most of all. His parents had paid the ultimate price for biology, he wouldn't fall prey to the same mistake.

Cade sank into the water as he considered his parents, murdered by the Mungons so long ago. The enemy clan had taken his parents in the hopes of destroying their clan and revealing the truth to the world. The Mungons wanted to take control of the entire world for the good of the shifter community, they said, but Cade knew better.They wanted to be the global rulers themselves. He wouldn't allow that.

The Mungons had used the very nature of shifters against his parents. Kept the pair apart so they pined until they died, souls starved of each other. When a shifter's soul mated, separation was dangerous, ultimately deadly. The Mungons had known this but they hadn't known the strength of the Alexander boys or their clan. For a long time, Cade denied his own biology and the facts of their magical world. He'd agreed with his brother Jadrian that the cold damp conditions of their cells, along with starvation, had killed his parents. But seeing how Kane had fought to stay with Damesha had opened his eyes. Only a soul-stirring love could do that. A love that could kill you.

The clan became stronger over time and Cade ruled in such a way that brought in new clan members. The Mungons had retreated for a time but now they were back. It probably wasn't the best time to bring in a bride but Cade needed a woman to keep the clan mothers at bay.

Jacqui would suit the purpose. Diving under the water one last time, Cade stood from the steaming hot water and reached for a towel. His body glistened as water dripped down his muscular back, over a tight round bottom, and down corded thighs. Cade spent a lot of time in business meetings but he also worked hard. His body showed just how powerful he truly was.

His face was chiseled into strong lines, his jaw strong and powerful. His nose was lean but suited his face and his eyes had made many a woman, and many a man, quiver. Black as night, his eyes were magnetic and drew people in, despite his cold exterior. He could look straight through a person, rendering them all but invisible, but they'd still tremble, wanting his gaze to see them once more.

A handsome man, Cade had little time for sexual entanglements and even less time for love. His family came first, then the clan. There was little room for anything else after that. Jacqui would be his bride in name only and that suited him just fine. It had to.

He wasn't sure how he was going to keep all of this from Jacqui but if she stood up to her part of the bargain, and so far she seemed like she would, then things would be fine. There'd be no questions asked, so no answers would have to be given.

Looking into the steamy mirror in the bathroom, Cade knew that his life wasn't normal. He should be getting married for love but that wasn't in the stars for him. His purpose was to serve his clan and if that meant marrying a woman colder than an ice cube in an Arctic freezer, then so be it. At least she was nice to look at. Clothed and ready to go, he shifted his head, trying to ease muscles that had become tense as soon as he stepped out of the bath. Time for battle.

Jacqui

Jacqui prepared for the dinner in her normal fashion. She ensured she was well dressed and that every hair was in place. She'd spent the day with Damesha and the baby, along with the ever wonderful Annie. It had been a very unusual day for Jacqui as she spent it dressed in a pair of jeans and a t-shirt. She hadn't worn jeans since the day Evelyn first took her shopping when she was 18 years old. It was an odd experience, even if the denim was smooth, expensive, and as soft as a baby's blanket.

Without her formal clothing on Jacqui felt exposed, as though she were almost naked. She kept looking down at herself, second-guessing her outfit. She spent a lot of time walking Annie, even though she had her own flap of a door to go in and out of the house. She also spent a lot of time gazing at a sleeping Elspeth.

"I'm so glad you told me the story of her name, Damesha," Jacqui said with an awkward smile. She was building something unusual for herself with Damesha; a real friendship.

"I'm hoping the book will be printed soon. I spent a long time getting it all in order and now Elspeth's story is going to be told." Damesha looked satisfied with life. A former slave, Elspeth's namesake had led runaway slaves from southern states to the free-state of Kansas before the Civil War freed those enslaved throughout the nation. A heroine that history forgot about until Damesha came along and dug up her story.

Jacqui found the woman fascinating. She'd overcome a life of parental drug use, the consequences of parental incarceration, poverty, and the death of her parents to succeed in her career. Now she had Kane and Elspeth. Jacqui wasn't sure if they were married or not but it didn't matter to her. She'd not asked Damesha a single probing question, the other woman had simply volunteered the information.

Damesha could be a problem in her ice wall. Jacqui had considered avoiding her but she'd suffered a new emotion when she refused a lunch invitation; she'd missed the triple threat of Damesha, Elspeth, and Annie. She'd answered the next offer with a quick yes.

Jacqui decided she'd let herself have this time with the trio as she was facing a pointless life, after all. As little more than an ornament, she was going to die and be forgotten the same as the first Elspeth had. Only there wouldn't be a young woman to bring her out of obscurity over a hundred years later. She knew that was the life she'd wanted, but the woman's story, along with Damesha, had made her wonder about the future.

Jacqui wandered down to the dining room and joined Cade. As usual, they were dining alone because Cade liked to eat late at around eight o'clock. He kept a hectic and varied schedule, something it would be Jacqui's duty to keep up with. She sat with her knees together and her hands in her lap as a young woman she still hadn't been introduced to served up their food. Roasted chicken tonight. At least the food was good. Well, it had improved since she'd learned to nail her ice wall up anyway. Cade could crack it sometimes, melt the ice to a glassy sheen, but she always managed to plug the faults before it gave way completely.

Suppressing the urge to sigh, Jacqui began eating and waited for the man to speak. She didn't do this out of fear of physical or even mental harm, it was just something she'd learned to do with him. He'd talk, eat, then go to bed or whatever it was he did at night. She wasn't concerned with that, only with making sure he was pleased with her. As usual, she spoke little.

"I think it's time to set a date, don't you, Jacqui?" He said the words casually, without inflection, as he said most things now.

"Of course. What day were you thinking of?" She cut up an asparagus spear before taking a small bite and looking at Cade.

"I thought perhaps Saturday. Then we can go on the expected honeymoon to New Orleans for a few days, perhaps. Then back home. Is that amenable?" He didn't even look at her.

"That sounds fine, I haven't been to New Orleans in a few years. It would be nice to go back."

"It's settled then." He went back to eating his food, the day's discussion over with it seemed.

The plates had been cleared and a dessert tray brought out once they'd finished the meal. They both made a choice and they were alone once more. Jacqui always felt strange about the staff or whatever they were. She knew nothing about them and they never spoke about anything other than the food. They also seemed to appear and disappear from nowhere. One moment they were there, the next they were gone.

"One other thing, Jacqui. Kane says you spend quite a bit of your day with Damesha and the baby. That's fine, no, don't worry." She'd been on the verge of saying she'd stop immediately if it was a problem but he stopped her. "No, I just wanted to tell you that if you'd like to, sometime in the future, we can adopt a child. If you'd like to. I know it was something we dismissed in the situation, having children, but I thought that maybe one day we'd both like to have a child of our own."

"Whatever you'd like, Cade." She'd considered the idea but hadn't fully thought about it. A child of her own? That was a big step.

"Good. I'll see you tomorrow then. I have to go out of town tonight, and I'll be back tomorrow evening.

Someone will come with dress samples for you in the morning." With that, he wiped his mouth and left the room.

Married and a mother, all within an hour. Finally allowing herself that deep breath she'd been putting off, Jacqui wondered if she hadn't bitten off more than she'd planned for with Cade. She had to fight hard to maintain her walls, she'd had to fight tonight to reach over and touch his hand. That warmth he'd shown on her first day here had disappeared, now he'd come to be the man she expected. She wished now she'd never seen that warm side of him.

Standing, she walked to her room to spend another quiet night alone. She'd taken up crocheting as a way to pass the time, and had started a blanket for the baby. Using local yarn from lambs' wool, she was excited to see the blanket taking shape. She'd made a few mistakes but that was part of the fun of the process, wasn't it? The act of crocheting might be the only place she'd ever allowed herself to make a misstep. Changing into a silk nightgown, she settled onto the white linen settee in her room and turned on some music. With a secret smile all of her own, she wondered if soon she'd be making one for her own child.

4

Jacqui

"He's nothing like your father, Jacqui, calm down." Jacqui stared into the mirror, alone for a moment in her room, and made a face at herself. All of her worries had surfaced as the day progressed. She was dressed in the mermaid style creation of silk, lace, and seed pearls that she'd bought as a sample size from the distributor and couldn't believe just how lovely she looked. This might be a sham wedding but she'd found her dream gown for it.

She hadn't thought it mattered but when she'd seen the dress she knew it was the one. Sexy but tasteful, demure but provocative, it was everything she wanted in a wedding gown. None of them had to know the virginal white was suitable to her status. Now she just had to calm her head and her stomach down.

Doubts had started as soon as she woke up. As the hairdresser spun her hair into a transfixing plethora of braids she knew would probably take her hours to undo, she told herself Cade wasn't a criminal. Unlike her father.

As Damesha helped her to slip the gown over some very expensive lingerie, she told herself Cade wasn't a cheat. Unlike her father.

As she took one final moment to look herself over, her makeup artist sweeping one last bit of blush across her cheeks, she told herself that Cade might be cold but he was honest. Unlike her father.

With shaking hands, she took her bridal bouquet from Damesha and walked down the stairs. A team of photographers took pictures of her as she trailed down, the popping flashes of the cameras making her dizzy for a moment. She stared into the cameras, her eyes round and wide, a pose that to her screamed of her fear but to others showed only innocence and curiosity. Some would even later say how hopeful she looked. Jacqui knew it was fear that told her she was wrong and Cade was just like her father.

Damesha held the train of the gown as she walked out to the bower prepared for the nuptials and Jacqui told herself that Cade might be many things, but weak and conceited weren't one of them. Finally, she stood before him, their hands joined, and she knew that this man might be the alpha male type and that he'd always want his way, but he wasn't her father. He was nothing like her father and could never be anything like him. Cade would never leave her to fend for herself; he'd never leave her in poverty with her only caretaker a drug addicted woman sinking into her own despair. He might not be her lover or her best friend, but he would be a great husband. She'd already signed the papers to prove it.

The rest of the actual wedding blurred past. Jacqui said the words required and looked ecstatic to be wedding Cade. All she could see was his eyes. For the first time since the day she'd met him his eyes held warmth. Even curiosity.

The only people present were his family, mainly his brother and Damesha, and a few people she didn't know but assumed were important. There'd been nobody she wanted to invite. Evelyn and Carla couldn't come on such short notice and she had no family that she knew of. A small reception was going to be held briefly, and an hour later they were heading to the airport to take a private jet to New Orleans.

"Thank you for coming." She air-kissed Cade's

brother on the cheek before looking to the next person in line; a tall older woman with badly dyed black hair and cold gray eyes.

"I know what you are," the woman said with acid in her voice before turning away.

Jacqui's eyes notched in confusion, wondering how the woman knew she was a fake bride. The woman disappeared before Jacqui could ask her. Damesha rushed up to Jacqui with arms open wide. She looked beautiful in a light blue silk dress.

"Congratulations!" Damesha hugged Jacqui close, an unexpected touch that Jacqui would normally have pulled away from but she couldn't disappoint the woman.

Jacqui wrapped her arms around the other woman and felt the almost robotic fog that had overtaken her begin to evaporate for a moment. She reveled in the touch and absorbed the warmth Damesha offered. Then she brought the wall down again and pushed the woman away gently.

"Thank you, Damesha. How's Elspeth?" The baby was with her adoring father.

"Kane! Bring Elspeth over, her new aunt wants to see her!" Damesha called out to her husband with a wide smile of pride.

Jacqui looked down at the baby, her light coffee-colored skin and blue eyes captivating her for a moment. "She is so beautiful."

"She is, thank you. I bet you're going to miss her aren't you?" Damesha's pride was still shining in her eyes as Annie came up to snuffle at her knees. "And our Annie. Hey, baby."

Damesha bent down to pet the dog, missing the moment of pain that flashed in Jacqui's eyes as she realized she was going to miss all of them. By the time Damesha stood back up the pain was gone, a calm look of resignation replacing it.

"I'll be expecting pictures every day! Let me find Cade now, I think we're going to eat soon." They hadn't wanted a drawn out wedding, just a simple affair to mark the occasion. If they were together too long questions might be raised about why they never touched or how they didn't appear to be in love.

Damesha already had her own questions, Jacqui had seen it in the woman's eyes, but so far she hadn't asked. Jacqui was grateful for Damesha's discretion and squeezed her hand before moving away. She found Cade directing the placement of food around the table and took her seat in preparation.

Everyone was soon gathered around and enjoying the food. As the sound of scraping forks and knives waned, Kane stood and held his champagne glass aloft.

"To the bride and groom, may you share a lifetime of friendship, happiness and love." A round of cheers followed the toast and Jacqui looked away for a brief moment. Her eyes were stinging again at the lie she was living.

She'd get used to it, she told herself. She had all she wanted now, right?

She drank two more glasses of champagne before the trial was over, the cake consumed, and her clothes changed. She and Cade, handsome in an all-black tuxedo, made their way out of the door as the gathered family and friends saw the couple off.

Jacqui ducked, trying to avoid getting sunflower seeds in her hair as the happy people behind her threw the birdfeed after them. She wondered in a detached way if any of the seeds would sprout later.

"Let me help you in." Cade took her hand and guided her, her tight white dress a little unbending as she tried to get into the long black car waiting for them. "You looked lovely today."

He slid in beside her and failed to see her look of shock at his words.

"Quite a lovely day, I must say, thank you." He flicked a button, letting the driver know they were ready and the car took off, speeding to the airport.

"You, uh, you looked very nice yourself. Thank you

for today." She sat stiffly beside him, not close enough to touch at all. Her hands rested in her lap, the picture of demure womanhood he'd wanted. Her hair was still in a multitude of plaits but it suited her. She'd take it all down later when he wasn't watching.

The driver took the bend out of their driveway rather sharply and Jacqui instantly felt the result of three glasses of champagne as she failed to react quickly. She landed in Cade's lap and his eyes caught hers. She was unable to move further, desire flaring instantly.

Stronger and hotter than she'd ever felt the need before, desire pulsed through her body as she came into direct contact with Cade. Her lips parted slightly, her nostrils flared, and her pupils dilated, matching the exact responses she saw in him. His eyes seemed to change, a light appearing in them she'd not noticed before. He leaned down slowly, his lips drawing closer and she couldn't move. Inside she screamed at herself to move away, to push him away, anything but stop him kissing her.

Jacqui couldn't stop it.

She closed her eyes, anticipating the moment, longing for it with all of her soul. She waited and hoped but nothing happened. She opened her eyes, confused.

Cade was still staring down at her but something else appeared in his eyes. Shock maybe? Horror? He pushed her away and she moved to her window, settling into the seat as her cheeks flamed. She'd revealed herself to him. And he'd rejected her. Shame filled her and she stared out of the window. He was gay, what had she been thinking?

She felt shame at her moment of obvious desire. What he must think of her! Okay, so he'd seemed to reciprocate for a moment, that didn't mean anything really. It could have just been curiosity.

"We'll be at the airport soon enough. You can nap if you'd like, there's a bed on board or have a shower. The flight shouldn't take too long." His voice was strained but she didn't look at him. She didn't want to reveal any more secrets to him today, not if she could help it.

She spent her wedding night, a balmy night in a private bed and breakfast in New Orleans, alone in her own room. She had no idea where Cade was. Sitting on a balcony in the long white negligee she'd bought herself in a moment of weakness, she watched the sun go down and wondered if she'd made the biggest mistake of her life.

* * *

THINGS DIDN'T CHANGE much after their wedding night. Cade spent most of his time on his phone or out, she had no idea where. She spent her time revisiting places she'd seen before or going to places she'd missed the first time around. Some were new and she loved the way the city was always adapting, rolling with the flow. She needed to be more like that, she decided.

She bought things for the baby with the credit card Cade had given her, and a few things for her room. Apparently, she was going to have her own suite of rooms in the house and bought some furniture from a merchant specializing in local woods. She also bought Cade something but had no idea when she'd ever give it to him. She found it in an antique shop, tucked away beneath a black velvet cloche hat from the 1920's. A man's ring, the stone carved from a large piece of amber, the ring was obviously old and detailed with scrollwork. In the spaces left were smaller pieces of amber filled with tiny bubbles and insects. Something about the ring caught her eye.

Taking it to the shop owner she waited for the woman to tell her the price.

"I'm sorry, there's no tag on this and I just don't remember it. Where did you find it?" The middle-aged woman with curly long blond hair and brown eyes looked at Jacqui inquiringly.

"It was under the black hat, on that marble side table

over there." Jacqui waved in the general direction of the table.

"Oh, I see. Well, normally I wouldn't sell this without finding out more about it but, well, there's something about you." The woman offered Jacqui a reasonable price and she paid with a thank you. She tucked the now boxed ring away in her bag, wondering if she'd ever really give it to Cade or if it would sit in her bag forever.

"Sometimes customers find things we miss. It's the strangest thing, stuff just appears from nowhere!" The woman gave a wave of her arms, a black silk shawl over her shoulders making the gesture more dramatic, and shook her head. Jacqui smiled and left with a word of understanding.

After a walk around a few other shops, Jacqui made her way back to the bed and breakfast and settled in for some lunch. Her phone buzzed just as the bed and breakfast's owner was taking the plate away.

"Hello?"

"Hi, Jacqui, it's Carla. How are you?" Her voice sounded uncertain, as though she'd been on the verge of hanging up the phone before Jacqui answered.

"I'm good, how are you?" It was nice to hear a familiar voice. She hadn't realized how much she'd missed the other woman until she called.

"I'm not doing bad, actually. It's been a while, things have changed, but I'm good." It hadn't really been that long but Jacqui knew well how quickly life could change.

"You went through with it then?" Jacqui's voice revealed her concern. She'd caught the "things have changed" part and knew what it meant.

"I did. But so did you. How is it?" Carla sounded concerned now too.

"It's, well, I just hope you enjoyed your experience." Jacqui didn't want to complain about something she'd worked towards, planned for.

"It was certainly eye-opening. I didn't think it would really change anything but it has. Some things make sense now anyway." Carla gave a light laugh.

Jacqui knew Carla wouldn't go into detail on the phone, the same as she wouldn't, but knew from Carla's voice that she was okay. Her voice had become stronger as she spoke.

"So you got married then? Congratulations."

"Thank you. It's been an experience as well." A boring one so far but she wasn't going to say that out loud, ever.

"Should I come to see you?" Carla's voice sounded almost teasing but the offer was there, nonetheless. Jacqui could hear a hint of hope in Carla's voice.

"That would be nice. I'll talk with Cade about it."

Jacqui was curious about that teasing note but she wasn't going to pursue it. She'd like to see her friend though. Any port in a storm, wasn't that the saying?

"Just let me know when. Text me the details and we'll arrange something. Take care sweetie, Evelyn's calling, I have to go."

Jacqui didn't even get to say goodbye, knowing Carla jumped when Evelyn called.

She was just putting her phone down when it started to chirp again.

"What did you forget?" A laugh escaped her as she answered.

"Pardon?" This was a different voice.

"Damesha?"

"Hey girl, I just thought I'd check on you. I guess Cade's staying busy and leaving you to explore the city in peace, huh?" She got right to the heart of the matter.

"Yes, you know Cade. How are you, honey?" Jacqui hoped to distract Damesha quickly. Her friend had finally stepped her toes into the waters of Jacqui's private life but at least she'd done it tactfully. Damesha let her off the hook and began telling her about Annie and Elspeth.

"Annie's decided she's Elspeth's mommy and won't leave her side. She hates the bathroom because that's where I bathe her so she usually has to be carried in there. But if Kane or I take Elspeth in there she follows us straight in! And she sleeps under Elspeth's crib. Annie's always slept at my feet until now. Well, sometimes beside me if there is thunder or she's not well, but always with me. Not anymore. My baby has stolen my dog!" Damesha laughed from the other end of the line.

"She's a mighty defender, that little girl of yours. I miss you all. I wish…" But she stopped herself before the words came out. She let the line go silent as she castigated herself for getting caught up in the moment.

"I know honey, you'll be home soon enough. I'll send you something shortly, keep your phone charged. I'm going to go, there's uh, I think Elspeth needs me." For some reason, it sounded like there was a puppy on Damesha's end. A madly barking puppy. Damesha quickly hung up the phone just as quickly as Carla had and Jacqui was left with nothing but the sound of a passing car to distract her.

She sighed and put the phone down. Just a few more days and she could go back to her crocheting, the trio of females that made her smile, and her empty life. Sipping at a cup of coffee that appeared at her elbow courtesy of the owner, she watched the sun as it raced across the sky. It refused to speed up no matter how hard she wished it to.

* * *

Jacqui placed the last of her bags in the trunk of the rented car and looked back at the bed and breakfast. She'd always found New Orleans magical, wonderful; a place she didn't really want to leave. She'd been happy to return, hoping it would chase some of her sadness away but it hadn't worked. Somehow being in the place she loved so much had made it worse.

Cade got into the car without a word and she followed him in, settling into the plush leather of the passenger seat. As the city passed her by, the morning sunlight almost blinding, she wondered if she'd ever return now. She'd only felt sadness here this time, emptiness. Suppressing an urge to sigh she settled in to playing the part of the aloof but happy new bride.

She wanted a drink but knew she'd have to wait for the flight. Jacqui looked out of the window as the streets passed them by, wondering why her purse felt so heavy. Looking inside of it, she found a bottle of her favorite rum, the rum she drank when she was alone. How did that get in there? Maybe the bed and breakfast owner had slipped it in before she left, she'd had enough of it from the woman's bar, after all. Making a mental note to send the woman a thank you card she settled back into her seat. Maybe she'd have a bit on the plane.

* * *

"I really don't know what else to do to fill my days. I think if I make Elspeth one more blanket you'll start to think I'm out to kidnap her." Two weeks later Jacqui was going stir crazy.

Cade had done his best to avoid her ever since they'd made it back to Kansas. She'd tried to join women's groups in town but there weren't any and the women she'd met so far were all cold and aloof, much like herself. Jacqui wasn't necessarily looking for tight bonds but she'd hoped to build some kind of working relationship with the community, to become a part of it and be an asset for her husband. Nothing like that existed out here.

She was having to come to terms with so much so quickly that her head was spinning.

"Are you sleeping better?" Damesha asked the question in an off-hand manner as she handed Elspeth over to her new aunt. Heading over to her own kitchen sink she started to wash vegetables for a salad she was making.

"Oh. Well. Not really." Jacqui had experienced days of nightmares when she first got back, the memory of the night her parents argued plaguing her mind. The dream replayed night after night but she could never make out what they were saying. It sounded as though she were under water and people above the water were screaming down at her.

In a moment of weakness, a moment that saw Jacqui falling asleep on Damesha's couch, Jacqui had confided her lack of sleep to Damesha. Now the dreams had shifted, from memories to things that could be if the world was a different place. A very hot place filled with beds and black lace.

Jacqui felt her temperature rising as the dream came back to her, the dream she'd had last night about Cade coming into her room and waking her, telling her he couldn't control himself anymore and that he needed her. Unlike reality Jacqui hadn't pushed him away but drew him to her, begging for his touch.

In her dreams, she was unrestrained, abandoned and demanding. She wished real life could be that way. Jacqui realized she'd come to be a totally different person from the cold woman who'd stepped off a plane not that long ago. Something about witnessing Elspeth's birth, her connection with Damesha, and the marriage had changed her.

Taking the glass of wine that appeared at the side of her hand, thanking Damesha quietly for the glass, she sipped and wondered why she'd changed. Alright, the things that had happened were pretty impressive but were they enough to make her go from a stone to a melting puddle of easily liquefied aluminum? Apparently so.

"Not really, huh? What's keeping you up?" Damesha had the salad ready and had chicken breasts grilling in a cooker. She still wasn't looking at Jacqui.

Jacqui felt a little less defensive when Damesha wasn't looking at her and sighed. Rocking the baby in her arms she wondered if this little girl had more to do with her present fluctuating state. Looking at the baby closer Jacqui realized she felt much heavier than yesterday and looked bigger too.

"Has she grown?" Jacqui's brow was crinkled down and she didn't catch Damesha's panicked look.

Damesha quickly picked the now sleeping baby from Jacqui's arms and carried her away, presumably to a crib or bassinet in the other room. Jacqui shrugged and picked up her phone, wishing she could text Carla. Or Cade. Those dreams were really doing a number on her self-control. She'd caught herself staring at his name in her contact list several times, on the verge of calling him. He hadn't changed though; there'd been no thawing whatsoever. She hadn't even seen him really since they got back, only in passing or at dinner, when he was totally silent.

"Girl, you can't keep doing all that sighing. You're

starting to bring me down and I have a wedding to plan." Damesha came in casting a castigating look at Jacqui. She turned the chicken breasts and Jacqui stared at her back, a little shocked.

"You're going to get married now? Why bother, Elspeth's already here." Jacqui knew something had prevented the two from marrying before the baby was born but hadn't been told what exactly, just that they'd needed to sort a few things out. Maybe one of them had been married already?

"Mainly just for my own satisfaction. It's a different world than it was 100 years ago but marriage still offers a security that domestic partnerships don't." Damesha's tone sounded stiff, as if she was being careful about what she revealed. Jacqui had noticed the woman did that sometimes but as she did it herself, she couldn't call her friend out for it.

"I suppose I know what you mean." She'd married a stranger for the same reason, hadn't she?

"So, about this not sleeping, maybe you should get some sleeping pills or something?" Damesha was trying to be helpful.

"I have them. They don't work. I think I need to just exercise more. I'm going to use the gym in the house this evening, run on the treadmill." She was a newlywed, Damesha was bound to wonder why she wasn't getting enough exercise but she knew the other woman was too tactful to ask.

"That sounds like a plan. And no caffeine before bed!" Damesha brought their food over to the table Jacqui had moved to while Damesha put the baby down and smiled at her friend. "Then we can talk about wedding stuff!"

Jacqui tried to smile but knew it was a poor attempt. She was having so many conflicting emotions she just couldn't muster the smile. She bit into her food, repressing another sigh. Maybe it was time to try to resurrect those walls again, she considered as she bit into the grilled chicken salad. It just seemed impossible to do around Damesha.

LATER IN HER BEDROOM, Jacqui started to really wonder about her decision and knew that, somehow, a part of Cade's life had escaped notice from the private investigator Evelyn used to inspect the client's life. She was in her room when a noise outside drew her attention. Normally cars were quiet, unassuming, and the kind that didn't draw attention. But as she sat reading a book, a loud but low rumbling came through the thick walls and intruded on the quiet she'd drawn around her like a blanket. Getting up from the sofa, she went to the window to see a long line of motorcycles filling the driveway. There must have been over eighty of them out there!

Stunned, Jacqui stood at the window and watched as one of the men got off of his bike and came to the door. A dark haired man dressed in the typical black leather pounded on the door and adjusted his privates, swiping a hand across his nose before jiggling the brass door knob. Jacqui felt a sneer form on her face as she looked down at the man. He wasn't handsome, far from it, and he looked like he needed a wash. She wanted to move away but she knew something was about to happen. Why else would so many people be with him?

Cade soon exited through the front door. His much taller stature and broader shoulders must have intimidated the other man because Snotty took a step down from the steps and went back to his bike. Cade looked down at the assembled people and spoke. Jacqui couldn't hear what he said because his back was facing her but she could read the other man's response. She'd learned to read lips as part of her training as a very special kind of escort and used the skill now.

"We ask for sanctuary, Cade. The Phlebos are working with the Mungons and their war is spreading. We don't want any part of it. We like secrets hidden away, just where they are, much like you and your clan. We'd like to seek shelter with you. The Mungons came and demanded we pay tribute and join them. We left and came here." The man, whose face was covered in facial hair, was hard to understand, but Jacqui caught the gist of most of it through the closed window.

She didn't see Cade's response but saw his shoulders tense and felt confusion as he shook his head no. The bikers with the man didn't look any more sophisticated than he did but they were asking for shelter. She couldn't believe he'd turn them away like that! Whatever this "war" was they needed refuge. But what if it's drugs? Maybe they're trying to draw Cade and his family into some kind of drug war? Jacqui tapped at her teeth with her thumbnail, anxious about the whole situation.

"What do you mean we've been killing your sheep? We haven't killed anything, we only just arrived today!" The shorter man stared up at Cade with anger and shock, his already tense body now straining towards Cade. "I think you ought to reconsider who you're turning down, Alexander."

The man's words made Cade stiffen this time but he held his ground. Jacqui knew that, ultimately, Cade would make the right decision. He might be cold, unapproachable and hard but everything he did was for his family. If he was turning these people down, it was for good. The man looked up at the window where Jacqui stood and a sick grin spread over his face. Jacqui stepped back into the shadows, feeling dirty just from the man's gaze.

"Who's that pretty little bitch?" The man pointed up at the window and Cade followed his finger to see Jacqui's window. His fist shot out and caught the biker just under his jaw on the right side. The man stumbled but instead of anger, he laughed as he steadied himself. "Somebody important then. Good to know. I'll remember this Alexander. All of it."

He gave a final pointing of his finger, this time directly at Cade, before getting back onto his shiny motorcycle to ride away. They drove around the circular area in front of the house and streamed down the driveway. Jacqui felt her anxiety rising and did a mental check of the pills she had. She might need an anti-anxiety pill before this day was over. She watched until the men were all gone then sat down. She realized her hands were shaking and clasped them in her lap. Something about the incident had shaken her and there wasn't anyone around to calm her fears. Maybe Cade was exactly like her father after all?

The thought terrified her and she pulled up her ice walls, hoping they were somehow much thicker than before. With a tilt of her head and a final look out the window, Jacqui decided it was time to regain control of herself. She couldn't afford to be weak in this house it seemed.

* * *

Cade

JACQUI WAS asleep when her door opened and a tall form crept into the darkness of her room. The figure walked quietly to her bed, their frame outlined by the light of her alarm clock. He paused, reaching to turn the clock around. The blue light was piercing.

The figure reached out to Jacqui's face, running a finger lightly down her cheek. He'd done this almost every night since she'd come to Kansas. Cade had even come to her room in New Orleans, though she didn't know about it. Now he was agitated, worried, and his finger twitched as he ran it down her hair, the silky strands too tempting not to touch. Jacqui moved in her sleep, rolling over to move away from whatever was pulling at her hair.

He saw her stiffen suddenly and knew she was awake. Uh oh.

He tried to sneak out of the door but she rolled over and turned on her light. He thought she'd scream, maybe jump out and hit at him, but she only stared up at him, her eyes clear but cold. He knew that no matter who or what he was, that's how she'd have met her fate —cold and collected.

For a moment he wondered what had happened in her life that made her so unemotional. He knew her past but he didn't have the full scope of each moment, of what she must have experienced or the impact those moments must have had on her in her file. Evelyn had provided the major events of Jacqui's life but that didn't tell him how her parents treated her, whether she was bullied at school, whether she was reclusive, ebullient, or just what most would call normal. He had no clue who he'd married.

At times like this, when he was stressed the most and wanted a confidant, a companion, he wished he'd taken a little more time to break down those walls of hers. He'd come in to check on her at night and longed to sit with her, to talk to her. He'd seen moments of tenderness on her face, especially around Elspeth and Annie. He wanted to see that look directed at him too.

"What do you want, Cade? Our contract says—" but he interrupted her before she could finish. She'd looked distressed for a moment, did she find him repulsive?

"There's a little problem I need to take care of. I just wanted to check on you. My apologies for disturbing you." He moved to walk away, to let her go back to sleep but she made a noise.

She cleared her throat while pushing her hair back. Looking up at him he caught the full brunt of her unguarded gaze and had to fight to hold back a gasp. "Do you want to talk about it?"

He almost said yes, he almost sat on the mattress beside her but he managed to wrestle his self-control back into place.

"No, it's uh, it'll work out I'm sure. No worries." Cade looked away from her as she sat up, her lace gown hiding little from his imagination. He felt as though he was a virgin once again, seeing a nearly nude woman for the first time. Shuffling his feet he started to walk away but she reached out for his hand.

"Why don't you stay? I saw those men outside earlier. They looked scary, who are they?" Her words were a plea for information, for comfort, and he felt them deep in his chest.

"They're bad news but nothing we can't handle. Just a gang trying to elbow into this area. We won't let them though. We've kept out worse things than that bunch." Cade stood at her side, looking down at her.

"Right. Why don't you take a seat then? I feel so, I don't know, small around you when you stand over me." She waved her hand at the side of the mattress where she moved to make room. He looked over at the sofa on the other side of the room but did as she requested.

"I have Kane and Jadrian out looking over the property, I suspect those people are camping on our land. I can't settle until they come back. Shall I ring for some coffee?" He picked up the phone to call the maid but she stopped him.

"Your brothers will keep an eye out, why don't you relax for a minute?" Her hand was still over his on the phone.

He looked into her eyes, the steel gray color captivating. He looked closely, at the way her slender nostrils flared, how the color rose into her high cheekbones. Her face was shaped like a heart, her chin small. She was beautiful. Was she aroused? He felt confusion, not sure of how to proceed. He didn't have to give her sex, that was part of their contract, sex was not necessary. But did she want him?

5

Jacqui

Jacqui stared into Cade's black eyes, the eyes she found almost disconcerting because they seemed to lack a pupil. She didn't know such eyes existed but she knew they were real, all three of the brother's had black eyes, all of them except the one that was adopted. She saw the tan skin of his face flush a red color as she stared at him.

His nose, fine but strong, not too large and not too small, flared now as her eyes dropped to the full dark lips above a strong chin. His cheekbones, sharp and pronounced, colored pink as a flush crept up his face. His forehead was broad but not too tall. In all, a handsome face with strong features that she longed to touch, to trace with her fingertips. But he was gay and wouldn't want her touch. Not a lover's touch anyway. Maybe they could be friends?

"Do you want to stay with me until Kane and Jadrian come back?" Jadrian was the adopted brother, Jacob the middle son, Kane the baby. She knew he'd be worried about them.

"That might be nice. But it could be a while, there's a lot of land to cover." He seemed to calm down with her words, the flush creeping out of his face as she settled back into her pillows.

It was nice to finally spend some time with him as a human being and not the husband she didn't know. What she knew about him came from a file, that was all. It would be nice to talk to him.

"I'm not going anywhere. I have so little to do I'm afraid I'm monopolizing your niece." She gave a soft smile as she spoke, a smile that showed how stressful it had been to have nothing to do.

"Maybe I could find something for you to do around here?" He hadn't meant to sound suggestive but the words came out that way. He looked away before she responded.

"That would be nice. I don't know what I could do

but I learn quickly." She felt awkward admitting she had no formal skills.

"We'll find something." He looked around the room, searching for something else to say.

"Do you want to watch a movie?" She felt the need to fill the silence but had no idea how to fill it. She didn't want to pry but she wanted to learn about him. His movie choice would tell her something about him anyway.

"Sure, what do you have?" He looked so uncertain she almost smiled. Big bad Cade looking like a little boy, it was too sweet.

"I have anything you want to watch. What would you like?" She got out her mobile and swiped at an icon. She looked up at him, waiting.

He told her a title and she searched the app. Finding it she saw the film was a historical movie about the Civil War. Interesting, a history buff.

"Found it, let me just turn the television on." Using the app she connected it with her television and started the film. A romantic history film. Oh my.

They settled into the bed together, Jacqui handing over several pillows before shifting to the other side of the king-sized bed. She felt tense, sitting next to him and slid down to a more comfortable position as the movie wound on. A three-hour movie meant a lot of position shifting. She didn't realize she was falling asleep as she watched the film, didn't realize that she'd rolled over to his warmth and thrown her leg over his hips until she jerked awake. How did that happen? She was awake one minute and waking up the next!

When she realized how she was sprawled across him she stiffened. Shit!

"I'm so sorry, I don't know what happened." She pushed against him, trying to roll away but he stopped her.

She heard, and felt, a low rumble, in his chest and realized he was chuckling. Was he laughing at her?

"It's alright, Jacqui, it's nice actually. Stay put." His hand pushed between her shoulder blades gently, lowering her back down to his chest. Her head fit perfectly below the top of his shoulder and she realized she'd never felt so comfortable in all her life. With a sigh she let the tension in her body go, and settled in.

She refocused on the movie and realized she had no idea what was going on now but tried to figure out what she'd missed. When Cade's hand went to her hair and started to twirl strands around his finger she tried not to let it show that she liked his touch. When his fingers went into her hair and started to massage the base of her neck she couldn't pretend anymore.

A soft moan passed her lips as she felt him hit a

painful spot. The pain soon left as his finger dug at the area, releasing the tension built up there. She heard a low sound in his chest and wondered what it meant.

As his fingers worked along her neck, down to the bare spot her gown left, tracing her spine, she shifted, trying to give him better access to her body. She moved her hand, rubbing down his stomach and across his hips. She felt something there, a hardness that she'd never felt before but could identify. He was aroused!

She sat up, looked at him in question. His face was impassive but she could tell he had his teeth clenched. She looked down his body until she could see the outline of his arousal in the soft pants he wore. Oh my.

She looked back up at him, totally confused.

"But I thought you were gay?" She couldn't pull the words back in after she spoke them.

He sat up, looking at her like she was crazy.

"What?" He sounded like a few expletives went at the end of that question.

"Evelyn told me most of the candidates were gay. You like knitting..." She trailed off; trying to remember what else had made her think he was gay. "You didn't want sex."

"I'm not gay, I promise you that." His words came out in a deep tone, the sound soothing to her nerves. He didn't sound angry just, well, amused.

"But, I don't understand." She looked down at her hands, not wanting him to see her self-doubt. How had she gotten it so wrong?

"I wanted a wife to keep my family quiet, they kept asking when I'm going to find a wife. I don't plan on fathering children of my own, I'll adopt but I don't want children of my own. I also don't like emotional entanglements. I just wanted a nice, platonic wife who would shut my family up."

"Oh." His words had been brutally honest and stole the words from her head. That explained a lot though.

"You're starting to change that, though." He pushed his hand back into her hair and turned her face to his. "If that's alright with you, that is."

"I…" but she didn't get to finish because he kissed her deeply, taking her lips with his. She moaned into his mouth, inhaling him as his tongue darted out to tease her bottom lip, asking her to open her mouth to his.

He rolled her over so she was on her back, his weight pleasant as his leg went between hers and his hands went to her flat stomach. She was beautiful in her white lace gown, and he looked down at her with an orange fire in his eyes. Why had she never noticed those colors before?

"You are perfection." His words took her breath away just before his lips found hers once more.

Her arms wound around his neck, holding him close as their bodies fused together. Her heat blended with his where their bodies touched, and she felt a burning need flame into a roaring inferno of desire. She tried to speak his name but he didn't stop kissing her for a long moment. She decided to explore him instead, now that she knew he wasn't gay. It was a relief, one she'd laugh about at some point, but for now, she just wanted to touch him.

She pulled the black t-shirt over his head, revealing his broad bare chest, a chest with a tattoo high on his left shoulder. She couldn't make out the pattern in the light from the television so she contented herself with exploring him with her hands. She ran her hands over his well-toned chest, slowly exploring the hard ridges of his pectorals and down his flat abdomen before moving back up. He moved over her, kissing her again, her lips tender now but welcoming as his tongue explored her hot wet heat.

Jacqui allowed her legs to fall open, cradling him. She'd never felt someone so intimately close to her and reveled in the sensation of his hard length pressing into her soft core. Her gown had ridden up over her hips, exposing herself to him but he didn't look, he was too captivated with her mouth still.

She opened her eyes, pulling away from him slightly.

There was a question she wanted to ask but was afraid the asking would break the spell in case he answered negatively. She wanted to know if they were going to make love but decided it was best to just let nature take its course. She shook her head and smiled away his own questioning look. She pressed her lips to his and let her walls melt away completely for the first time.

She felt heat running up her spine, making her hot and shivery, and she couldn't stop herself from moving. He'd barely even touched her and she was on fire! Taking a shaky breath, she pulled her head away and tasted the skin just below his ear, her lips brushing lightly before she darted her tongue out for her first taste. She tasted his cologne and beneath it his scent, the wintery-woodsy smell now hot and spicy.

"Mm, you taste nice." She let her head fall back, wondering what he'd do now. Would he leave her or would he dare to take it further? She hoped he'd take it further.

"Let me taste you then. I bet you taste of cherries and cinnamon. Sweet and tangy, spicy and exotic." He brushed his nose along her neck, down the neckline of her gown, and back up the other side. His fingers trailed along, his lips grazing her flesh, making her shiver once more.

"Oh." She gasped the word, all but breathless as his

hot breath danced over her neck, to the same spot just below her right ear. She held her breath as she waited, wondering what his kiss would feel like there. The air exploded from her lungs when she felt the moist heat of his open mouth sucking at the spot. Her legs twitched, clasping around his hips.

"Cade." She cried out his name, not sure why but knowing she didn't want him to stop.

Not this time. She wanted it all. Men had tried to touch her before, to entice her into their arms but she'd always danced away, refusing their advances. Most of her clients didn't bother her but a few had tried their hand with her. Now she wanted it all, the touches, the kisses. All of it.

This man was her husband, but more than that he was a fire she couldn't resist. From the first moment she'd seen him, she'd been unable to get him out her mind. She pushed herself into him, up to his hardness, up to the soft pressure of his suctioning lips, up into the hand that had cupped her breast, kneading the soft peak in his overfilled palm. She could feel her nipple, hard and throbbing, pulsing beneath his grip, and longed for more. His tongue scraping against it, his fingers rolling it softly, then harder.

"Cade, please." She wanted more. She wanted the pictures burning through her mind.

He answered her plea and shifted once again, down to the mound filling his hand. He moved the fabric away and met skin just as silky as her gown. Her skin was a pale color, often protected from the sun, and he licked his lips as she watched, his darkness against her paleness somehow erotic. When his lips found her nipple, sucking the rosy bud into his mouth, she stopped thinking, stopped worrying that he'd stop, and pressed herself into his mouth. She wrapped her legs tightly around his hips and pushed into him as pleasure rocked down to her core.

Her hands moved along his body, wanting only to urge him into action, into being inside of her. With sudden awareness, she knew he was exactly what she needed. She craved him, and pushed at his sleep pants, wanting them to disappear. She made a soft sound of frustration when the waistband moved but would not budge. They were too close together for the pants to do anything more than reveal the tight round globes of his ass. She clasped at the muscled flesh, pushing him into her as she ground against him.

"Cade." She breathed his name again, her desperation on show.

She could feel the dampness she was producing, could feel the sudden pulsing of her inner muscles, and knew all she wanted was Cade plunging into her in that moment. She shifted, trying to remove his pants, and he followed her lead by moving away just long enough to kick the pants away. Before she could protest, he was back between her thighs, his fingers exploring her folds, seeking out the evidence of her desire.

He found her silky moisture, and plunged his fingers into her, two long tapered fingers diving into her most secret place. She thrust to meet the intrusion, delighted at the touch. She knew what sex was, she'd read about it, watched films, she'd just never done any of it. Now she had the one man she couldn't resist between her thighs, making her ready for his invasion.

With a grunt of satisfaction, he moved over her, his hand guiding his hard length to her opening. She felt his length, hot and pulsing against her core and opened wider for him. With a sure movement, he stroked his way into her, going deep and fast into her virginal body. He looked confused for a moment and she gasped as she felt a tearing sensation. He stopped to look down at her, shook his head slightly, and began to move.

Jacqui clung to Cade, her mind exploding with thoughts. She'd felt a twinge of pain but then her muscles relaxed around him. It felt strange to have him inside of her, to feel him pulsing within her as the blood flowed through his organ. When he began to move, she caught her breath. The sensation of him stroking her inner walls was exquisite, mind-blowing. She'd waited her whole life for this moment. She'd begun to think it would never happen but now she was glad she'd waited.

Cade moved slowly at first, letting her get used to him, then sped up, his eyes boring into hers. He didn't speak, he just moved.

She couldn't stay quiet though and began to speak to him, to urge him on. She wanted to know what it all felt like. Just in case it never happened again.

"Harder." She demanded, her eyes closed as she concentrated on the way her pleasure shifted with his movements.

"Oh God, deeper." He went deeper, tilting her hips slightly as he knelt between her thighs.

"Oh Cade, deeper. Oh God, deeper." She wasn't sure that was exactly what she wanted but she knew she needed more.

He pulled her legs up against his chest, holding onto them as he pulled her bottom from the mattress, thrusting into her deeper as she demanded.

She hung there, unaware of whether this was a good way to have sex or not but knowing that it felt right, it felt oh so good.

"That's it, oh yes, that's it!" She panted the words feeling something quivery and pulsing starting low in her abdomen, within her velvety inner walls, and screamed his name as the world exploded.

She rode the waves, unaware that he was watching her with interest, or that the noise piercing into her stupor was her own voice.

He waited for her to stop writhing, for her back to stop arching, for the keening to stop before turning her over onto her hands and knees.

She turned, boneless and eager to please, thrusting back at him as he brushed his hand lovingly over her round bare bottom. She heard him give a deep sound of satisfaction as he pressed into her. She pushed back, taking him in one stroke, her body still quivering from her release but starting to hum again. She wanted to lift up to that place again, to those eternal moments where the world was dark and quiet, to the point where she felt good, oh so good.

Cade arched over her back, his fingers finding her clit, her moisture making the button slick as he pressed into it. She gasped, her own hand going over his. The sensation was too much but he kept his finger there, a slow circling motion almost too much to bear. But then it sent heat out into her limbs, a buzzing sensation starting in her ears as he thrust into her and she rushed headlong down that dark tunnel into ecstasy once more.

She came apart in his arms, panting, wordless, but

moaning her pleasure as he thrust into her, hard, deep and fast. Her walls sucked at him, massaging him into tipping over the edge.

Jacqui came back to earth as he found his own release, the pulsing of his length inside her its own pleasure. She gasped with each inner explosion, hyper aware of the strangled sound that escaped him as he found his own pleasure.

She knelt there, taking his final thrusts and felt something crack inside of her. Something had been released and her whole body shook with it. Dropping to the mattress, she felt as though she were flying apart, as though her whole being had become little more than stardust. What was happening to her?

Cade, unaware that anything was happening, fell to the bed beside her and pulled her into his arms. He held her speechless form, kissing her hair, as he waited for her to speak. His fingers caressed her stomach, loving the gentle way her flesh curved as his fingers flowed from her hip to her stomach, a gentle roundness that his fingers enjoyed stroking.

Jacqui felt as though she'd spent years inside her quaking world but soon the sensation released her. She breathed heavily, almost panting as she regained something like consciousness. Something had changed and it was more than her. She looked up at Cade and for a moment saw the flickering of animal images. She stared at him, dazed, and something inside of her screamed a word she didn't quite understand. Not because it was a foreign word, or a word she'd never heard but because it simply made no sense. What the heck did 'shifter' mean?

6

Jacqui

A slow, wet, slide of a finger between her nether lips woke Jacqui in the early hours of the morning. The sky was just beginning to lighten as she pushed back into her husband's arms. He was touching her again and she couldn't believe she'd get to feel it for the rest of her life.

Pressing her head back into his, hoping his lips would find that spot on her neck again, she writhed her hips in time with his fingers, unable to stop her movement. Sweet, slow pleasure was burning from her center and she didn't want it to ever stop. She wound her arm behind her, seeking out his length, the sensation of him hot and filling her hand making her breath suddenly shudder in her chest. Oh, she loved this, she loved it so much.

"Good morning, Cade," she whispered, not wanting to break the spell he was casting.

"Good morning, princess." He growled the words just below her ear, his breathing as erratic as hers as she stroked him in her hand. He pushed himself into her hand, and she squeezed him tighter.

"I love feeling you sliding in my hand like that. You're so—oh!" She had to stop speaking, his finger was pressing harder into her clit, circling the nub faster.

"You were saying?" He prodded her to continue, his voice held expectation of an answer.

"I...oh Cade." She couldn't think, not with him talking to her, filling her hand, and touching her so intimately. "I... oh fuck."

She'd never said that word before but it seemed appropriate now, in his arms.

"Oh yes, I intend to fuck you, princess, but not before you come in my arms again. I love watching your face as your pussy sucks at my cock, pulling me deeper into your wet depths."

Jacqui shuddered once again, her body tightening in expectation, her breath stilled in her chest in anticipation as he continued to speak.

"I'm going to watch you come and then I'm going to

fill you with what you've got in your hand. And I'm going to make you mine again as I fill you with every inch of my cock." His words were low, hot, and shivered over her pebbled skin.

"Cade…" She gasped his name before she flew apart, her body and mind racing into a dark world where nothing mattered but the exquisite sensations flowing from his finger and into her.

Jacqui didn't have that weird moment she'd experienced last night and didn't care, she was too busy enjoying her husband fingering her into a quivery mass of nerve endings.

"That's it, baby, let it go. Let the whole world disappear because in just a few moments I'm going to slam into you and make me your world." His words were rough but made her shudder even harder, her body responding to his words of possession as though she'd been born to serve him.

She'd never wanted a life like that; devoted to a man, to love, a slave to her emotions. She'd only wanted peace and tranquility but Cade offered more than love, he offered a drug she could not resist. His sex.

And true to his word, Cade lifted her leg just as she was coming back down to earth and slid into her from behind as he held her leg up. She jerked with awareness, the sensation of him sliding into her different this way.

It felt more intimate than before, somehow. It felt like he was entering all of her, and she couldn't stop the shiver that passed through her.

She pushed her sex into him as she bent forward. His hand went to her waist, holding her still as he fucked her, letting her feel his length piercing into her and opening her with slow but steady friction. She savored the sensation of being split open before he started to slide out of her, the head of his cock now pulling her walls apart.

Cade took his time, she noted, letting her need build up once more as she tried not to move, wanting to let him do as he pleased. Jacqui opened her eyes, seeing their reflection in the mirror beside the bed. The sky was light enough to make out his eyes now, but most of the room was still in shadow. Her eyes met his and she saw a flash of orange in the dark depths for a moment. She couldn't look away and saw that her own gray eyes seemed to be sparkling with a shine she'd never really noticed before. Was this the haze she'd remembered seeing in her mother's eyes when the other woman had been stoned?

No, this was a deeper shine, a sparkling twinkle she'd never seen in anybody's eyes before. A deeper, harder thrust by Cade refocused her attention and she moaned her pleasure.

"Open your eyes, princess, look at us."

She did as he said, seeing herself spread open as he pulled her torso back up to his. She could see his length sliding into her and her lips parted in awe. Oh, that was gorgeous, watching him slide in and out of her, the wetness on his cock coming from her pulsing body. It was beautiful.

"You see me fucking you, filling you? You're mine." The low words were accompanied with a nip of her neck, his dark eyes boring into hers as he did so.

"Yes, Cade." He was an alpha male after all.

"Say it." He growled the words, demanding she obey.

"I'm yours, Cade, only yours." She gave into him, her will, her independence, her everything now attuned only to him and to his needs. He needed her to be his and so she was.

His hips started a tighter pace then, faster, not as deep, as he sought his own release inside of her, his movements only for his pleasure. But Jacqui felt her own pleasure building. She watched him behind her, pressed up onto his elbow, and let her hands slide to her own body.

One hand went to her left nipple, cupping her breast as her fingers clasped around the dark bud. The other went down to her clit and she exploded just as the first jet of Cade's release pulsed into her. Her fingers tightened on both buds, and she called out his name as she found her own release once more, coming with him as he groaned in satisfaction.

With a final grunt, Cade released her and went to his back. Jacqui stayed where he'd left her, shocked at her emotions, at the swelling of emotions in her chest. This wasn't supposed to be happening, not at all. He didn't reach out for her and soon he was snoring once more. Jacqui eased herself from the bed, knowing she wouldn't get back to sleep now, not with this new worry in her mind and heart.

As she'd come back to reality she'd realized that she was becoming overly fascinated with the man, that she might even feel some kind of love for him. But she barely knew him! She rarely even saw him, what was this incredible pull then? Was it love, this animal magnetism? She had to get out of the room, away from him, so she could think.

She went into the bathroom, her own private room, and started the water running into the porcelain tub. An old fashioned claw-footed tub, the thing was huge with a slanted back that allowed her to rest in a rather heavenly way. Jacqui loved the tub with the brass fittings. It suited the large white room filled with blood red towels, the only color in the room besides the brass fittings. A large round window with frosted glass allowed the sunlight to shine in, filling the room with warmth as the hot water filled the room with a haze.

Jacqui slid into the water, her tender body relaxing in a pleasurable way as she slid beneath the depths. Sighing loudly, she sank down to her chin and let her head fall back on the pillow she'd found wrapped in plastic when she'd first come to the house.

Jacqui knew she was trying to avoid her worries over Cade, her brain almost erratic as she tried to avoid over-thinking recent events. She knew she had to think about it all though and as she floated in the water, her pale body absorbing all of the heat it could, she wondered if she was in trouble here. She was meant to offer Cade comfort, but as the cold automaton he'd ordered as his bride, not this whimpering mess of "fuck me".

Jacqui couldn't decide if she was more put out with her willingness to give up her self-control to the man or with her need for him. She'd come into this with an idea, a plan. It had all gone out of the window the moment he'd touched her. What were things going to be like now? Was she going to have to act like a real wife? Could she allow people to see her so very sappy in public the way Kane and Damesha were?

She felt a shudder chase down her spine and shook her head no.

"That will not happen." She had too much reserve to ever allow that. Surely?

Jacqui tried to remember exactly how all of this had happened. They'd gone to New Orleans and all was well, she thought. There'd been a bit of a slip just after the wedding when she'd been thrown against her handsome husband in the car, but the moment had passed. Then she'd found that ring and had to buy it for him. She couldn't explain why she'd had to buy the ring at the time but she realized now that the orange of the amber matched the flashing in his eyes when he was aroused.

How had she gone from calm, cool and collected, to this? Jacqui let the hot water wash away her thoughts for a moment. Resting under the water, she expelled the air from her lungs and enjoyed the absolute silence for a moment. Sliding back up to breathe, she started her bathing routine and got out of the tub.

The thought of Cade still in her bed, warm and soft in sleep, made her want to crawl back into bed with him but she made herself dry her hair and wrap up in a towel first. Patience, you must be patient, she kept repeating to herself, in the hopes of not making a fool of herself. She opened the door of the bathroom and stepped into her room, his name dying on her lips before she spoke it.

Cade wasn't in her room. Her bed was empty. He hadn't even said goodbye! He'd just left.

Frowning at the door, Jacqui felt a sting begin in her chest. Was this how it was going to be? Late night passion, all day cold fronts? Maybe it was for the best. With her lips pressed together and her left eyebrow raised, Jacqui decided to finish her toilette, then go find some breakfast. Her pale eyebrow was almost translucent before she put her makeup on but it still managed to give off an air of irritation.

Things weren't going as she'd planned but in the burning light of day she knew there wasn't much she could do. She'd agreed to be his wife in name only but now, well now it was anybody's guess. Perhaps he'd never mention it again, maybe it was a momentary lapse. But she could still hear him growling the word "mine" into her ear as he came inside of her and she couldn't stop the shivering. Or the hope that she'd hear that word in just the same way again.

HOURS LATER, Jacqui stared out her bedroom window and realized she felt like a bird in a cage. Looking out at the life going on around her she wondered if she could really keep this up. Damesha and Kane were taking Elspeth out to some swimming hole thing and Jacqui hadn't made friends with anyone else yet. She was on her own and all she could fill her time with was watching the workers keep the grass mowed and the hedges trimmed.

She realized she felt like a fairytale princess locked away in a castle. Her clear eyes watched the people talking amongst themselves, the arrival of cars another curiosity. They didn't look happy to be there but their faces changed when the doors opened to the house. Perhaps Cade should know about that. She hadn't heard a peep from him the entire day, not a single word. She didn't even know for sure that he was in the house.

She was warring with herself, trying to make a decision about telling Cade about what she'd seen when her phone started to buzz. She ran to it, happy for the distraction, and smiled when she saw it was Evelyn.

"I don't know why you're calling but I'm so happy to see your name, Evelyn! How are you?" Jacqui knew she sounded as though she'd been running a marathon but couldn't help it, she was so happy to talk to her mentor.

"I'm at the airport honey, I just wanted to know if I could meet you this evening? We have some things to discuss." Evelyn didn't sound like her normal self, she sounded almost motherly and intense. At least that's the impression Jacqui got.

"Of course, where are you staying? Come to the

house, we have plenty of room." Jacqui would have insisted but Evelyn declined.

"It might be hard for you all to explain who I am and I'm sure your new husband doesn't want his family to find out what line of business I'm in. No, I'll stay in the roach hotel the town has listed. It won't be the first time I've had to stay somewhere like that. Shall we meet there at seven?" Evelyn didn't sound as though she expected Jacqui to decline so Jacqui didn't disappoint her.

"I'll be there then. I'm so glad you're here!" Jacqui knew she was probably worrying Evelyn with her ebullient happiness at hearing her voice but couldn't help it. She was changing and this was one of the signs of that change. It remained to be seen whether that change was for the better or worse.

Jacqui went to her closet, she had a couple of hours to get ready but she couldn't sit still. She drew out a pair of jeans but put them back for a pair of slacks. She could get away with slacks and a blouse, even if the town was tiny with few women dressing in anything more formal than their "fancy" jeans. With fresh makeup and her hair smoothed back into place, Jacqui went downstairs to find out about going into town. Usually, someone drove her but she had no idea when she'd be back so she wanted a car she could drive.

She went to Cade's office and knocked, unsure if he was even in the room or not.

"Come in." Well, that answered that. She gave a nod of her head and opened the door.

"Ah, Jacqui. What do you need?" Cade didn't even look up from his keyboard as he typed. How did he know it was her?

"Oh. Uh, a friend from Florida has come in for a visit. I'm going to meet her in town. I need a car."

"I'll have Kane drive you." Again he didn't look up. That was making her nervous.

"No, that's not necessary. Really. I could be a while, she's like my surrogate mother, my mentor. I could be gone a while." Her voice shook slightly at the end and she cleared her throat.

"I see, Evelyn's in town. If you don't want to bring her here that's fine but I'd prefer someone drive you into town. I'll call Kane now." He picked up the phone and Jacqui might as well have disappeared. She backed out of the room, shock coursing through her.

She went out to the front steps, waiting for her brother-in-law. She was warring with herself again, was she angry or hurt. Perhaps both in equal measures. She was angry that he'd just dismissed her without even looking up at her and hurt for the same reason.

Jacqui had tried not to hope for a warmer reception

from Cade, but she had and now she knew; her walls had to go back up. She doubted there'd be a repeat of last night's performance and dashed away her plans for new lingerie. She put away her burgeoning hopes for a family and a normal life. Cade wasn't that kind of man and she certainly wasn't the woman for that life either.

Kane pulled up and Jacqui slid into the town car with surprise. Elspeth and Damesha were in the back seat.

"We thought we'd go out and have a bite to eat while you're out, see what's happening in town." Damesha spoke but it was the look Kane sent his wife in the rearview mirror that let Jacqui know Cade had asked them to stay near her. But why? He acted like the family was constantly under threat but he'd never explained *why*.

Jacqui wanted to ask Kane what was going on but knew she'd get the same kind of brush-off answer Cade would give her. This family had secrets and she wasn't part of it enough to be let in on them yet. Feeling fear tighten her stomach for a moment Jacqui knew she'd have to change that somehow.

Damesha filled the drive-time with tales of Elspeth's doings that day and Jacqui let her friend distract her, asking the appropriate questions and making the right sounds. She really did adore the baby and Damesha so it wasn't a chore to listen to her, but Jacqui had a lot on her mind.

Namely Cade.

Kane soon pulled up to the tiny hotel Evelyn was staying at and waved her off as they headed to a restaurant across the street. She and Evelyn weren't going to have much privacy if they went there to eat. Which made her realize Cade probably arranged that as well. She hadn't even thought about it but now she knew the only reason Cade hadn't forbid her going out completely was because Kane and Damesha would be close by. With a roll of her eyes and a sigh, Jacqui went to Evelyn's door and knocked.

"Hi there, honey." Evelyn's soft southern twang soothed Jacqui's nerves and she smiled at her mentor.

"I am so glad to see you." Uncharacteristically, Jacqui took the woman into her arms and held her close rather than giving the usual stiff-armed clench with air kisses.

Evelyn searched Jacqui's face as she stepped away, letting the door close behind her. Jacqui tried to look away but Evelyn held her still.

"Not going as planned, huh? I thought it might not be." Evelyn went into the tiny kitchenette the hotel had installed in the room and began unpacking bags of what looked like Chinese food. Adding it to pots and pans, Evelyn soon had it all reheating.

"You brought my favorite with you? You're kidding me! Can you read my mind or something?" Jacqui kicked her heels off and found tableware, setting the small table in the room. "That's a great idea, my in-laws are at the place next door."

Setting the food down on the table, Evelyn sat opposite the younger woman and offered her the spoons. Jacqui filled her plate with her favorites: Szechuan chicken, an egg roll and fried rice. Evelyn handed over an unopened bottle of soy sauce and Jacqui indulged herself in the one food she could not resist. They ate in silence for a few moments but as the initial wave of excitement wore off Jacqui looked up at Evelyn.

"Why are you here?" She knew she had to be the reason but wasn't sure why.

"Things have changed for you, Jacqui. Some very profound things. I thought I'd check in on you." Evelyn's eyes probed Jacqui's but the gray eyes of the young woman were resistant to her probing as usual. Jacqui had always been an impenetrable fortress.

"They have, yes. Some of it is confusing but I don't think there's anything you can do about it." Jacqui sighed but then smiled as she realized that somehow Evelyn had snuck her favorite butter pecan cheesecake on the table as well. "How did you do that? I swear stuff just keeps appearing. People have some serious sneaking skills."

"That's one of the things that I came to talk to you about but I'm not sure you're exactly ready to hear it all." Evelyn pushed her plate to the other side of the table and started cutting the cheesecake, putting two slices on smaller plates. She wouldn't look Jacqui in the eye this time.

Jacqui paused as she raised her fork to her mouth, the last bite of her rice on her fork. "What?"

"Well, are you sure people are sneaking things to you?" Evelyn stared down at her pie, really enjoying eyeballing it for some reason. Jacqui thought it might melt Evelyn was staring at it so hard.

"Of course I am, how else would things keep popping up?" Jacqui took her first bite of the pie and moaned, it was just so good.

"I didn't bring this pie, Jacqui." Evelyn's words came out as a mutter and Jacqui didn't hear her.

"Pardon?" Jacqui looked up.

"I didn't bring this pie." Evelyn spoke louder, looking at Jacqui finally.

"Of course you did. Don't be silly. How else would it have gotten here?" Jacqui thought it was a bit silly to try and trick her but thought Evelyn had to be making an attempt to. How else had the pie got on the table?

"What else has shown up, Jacqui?" Evelyn was quiet but her words reached Jacqui.

"I guess, well, mainly coffee and food. It's always showing up when I'm thinking about it. Usually just a passing thought but then there it is. People really are sneaky, Evelyn, I don't know how they know what I want but maybe it's intuition?" Jacqui still wasn't putting any stock into what Evelyn had said, thinking she was joking.

"Nothing else?" Evelyn reached over to Jacqui, making her look up.

"No, just food and drinks." Jacqui finally looked up at Evelyn again with concern. What was going on here?

Evelyn waved her hand and the dirty dishes and empty bowls disappeared, the cheesecake moving to the center of the table as a candle appeared.

Jacqui's eyes went wide and she moved back in her chair, sitting up straighter.

"What the heck?" She looked at Evelyn in astonishment. "How did you…"

"I'm a witch, Jacqui, the same as you." Evelyn danced her fingers around, flower-filled vases appearing wherever her fingers pointed with a tap. "Are you sure you can't do this?"

Jacqui watched the room fill with roses, peonies and orange blossoms. The smell became too strong after a few moments and Evelyn swiped her hand at the room, everything but two vases of orange blossoms disappearing. Jacqui's head was swimming. The sights, the smells, far too much for her to take in.

"What else…whoa…I need to lie down." Jacqui wobbled over to the bed, falling down onto the hard, thin mattress. The mattress squeaked in protest but Jacqui didn't care, the camel's back had just broken.

"It'll pass, honey, I promise. It's just shock." Evelyn came to sit beside of the young woman she felt was almost her daughter. "Your mother bound your powers when you were a baby, but she apparently set a spell to free you when you married the man you were going to spend the rest of your life with."

Evelyn stopped with a sigh of sadness. Stroking Jacqui's pale blond hair, she looked down at her stricken face. "I know this is a lot to take in so I'm not going to leave for a few days but there are things you have to know, my dear. Things we need to arrange. It's not typical for a witch's powers to be bound as long as yours have. You may never gain your full powers or you may get them all of a sudden. You have to be ready."

Jacqui could only look up at her mentor in confusion. She knew it was true, she'd seen the evidence with her own eyes. But to believe she'd be capable of those sorts of things?

"Whoa." It was all Jacqui could think to say.

"I know, honey. I know."

"So… why? Oh, why didn't Mom use her powers then? It obviously comes from her. Dad would have used it all selfishly, we'd never have had the life we had if he'd been a witch. Whatever. Why didn't Mom save us from that life?" Jacqui's words came as they occurred to her, erratic and fast, one thought leading to another.

"Your father used her up. He insisted she bind your powers so he could save them for later but he used hers up. I tried to warn your mother, I tried to stop their union but, well, you can't stop a young witch from doing as she pleases. And she had you. Binding your powers greatly decreased hers and soon after your father was investigated. Getting him out of all that finally broke your mother's powers. She couldn't save you and she couldn't unbind yours." Evelyn was still stroking Jacqui's hair, hoping to ease the pain the words were bound to be causing.

"So every bit of it was my father's fault? He created our downfall?" Jacqui's eyes were dry but she felt the sting of tears in her nasal passages. Her eyes just refused to cry any more for that man.

"Basically. When I found your mother she was heading down a rough road. It's not often we find magical children abandoned, your mother came from a good family to begin with. She retained some of her refinement and I thought I could save her. She found your father instead. I often wonder what would have happened if I'd left her on her own." Evelyn sighed and produced two glasses of scotch with lemon and ice. She handed one to Jacqui as she sat up.

"I have a feeling my father was in her future no matter what path she took. That man was like a plague." Jacqui sipped at the strong drink, letting it burn down her throat smoothly.

"I suspect you're right. That's part of the reason I'm here. Cade cannot know about this." Evelyn wouldn't meet her eyes again, Jacqui noticed.

"I understand. Believe me, much better than you may know. I saw what my father did to my mother. To me. I won't allow that to happen to me." Jacqui's back straightened and her face tightened.

"That's my girl." Evelyn patted Jacqui's shoulder and sighed again. "I guess that's all for tonight really. All I had to tell you anyway. What do you have to tell me?"

"Nothing really. Our relationship has become sexual, things are weird, but a lot of that is just who we are. We're both reserved people." Jacqui went back to pick up the cheesecake.

"I'm going to eat this, then I'm going home." She smiled at Evelyn who came to sit with her.

"Not on your own you aren't. You'll be sick as a dog, honey. Let me help."

The two spent another hour discussing Jacqui's life since she'd moved to Kansas and what she might expect over the coming weeks. Evelyn also gave her the contact information of a professional witch teacher, a woman who usually taught children but occasionally picked up the occasional stray. Evelyn gave Jacqui one more warning before she left, her arms tight around the young woman.

"You must not tell this secret, Jacqui. I know you know the consequences but I have to give you that warning. Keep this to yourself and try not to reveal yourself. It's absolutely important."

"I understand, Evelyn. I'll see you tomorrow." Jacqui walked away from her friend and watched as Evelyn shut the door. Her entire life had just changed. Again.

7

Cade

Cade watched his wife leaving and rubbed his left hand over the back of his neck. He had no idea how to handle the current situation. Oh, he knew how to keep her safe, but keeping her out of his head was a totally different matter. The Mungons and their plans were a problem he had to soon deal with but for now, his wife pushed everything else out of the way.

"They're in the woods then?" Cade turned back to his brother Jadrian, the man the exact opposite of Cade and his other brothers.

"Yes, we've found fifteen slaughtered cows so far, all torn to shreds. It's the wolves." Jadrian's smooth voice was low and warm, a contrast to the icy coldness of his light green eyes and blonde hair. More golden than Jacqui's platinum. Jadrian's hair fell into his eyes. He always needed a haircut.

"That fucking motorcycle gang of werewolves. Why did they have to come here!" It wasn't really a question and Jadrian didn't bother answering.

"I have men out with the herds now. I expect they think they can do as they please, they're used to being the big dogs over in California." Jadrian waved his drink in the general direction of the state.

"They haven't met shifters then. Not our kind that turn into whatever we choose when we choose. Take them out. I'm not having this in our territory. Take out any you find stalking our cattle." Cade rubbed the back of his neck once more, not looking forward to more battles but he knew a war was coming. The Mungons were pushing the entire magical world into it.

"I'll see to it."

"Jadrian," Cade called out to his brother before he could walk out of the door.

"Stay away from the Phlebos. They're trouble."

"I can handle it. I promise."

"All the same, keep Jacob with you from now on. He's level-headed, he'll keep you out of trouble." Cade's tone brooked no argument and Jadrian hung his head.

"Sure, Cade."

Cade knew his brother couldn't be into drugs but Damesha had seen Jadrian's death. Cade had to try to prevent that as well. Fuck, he thought, it's too much. Where's Jacqui?

He wanted to lose himself in her arms, between her thighs. The hurt look in his brother's eyes as he left was another dart into his armor, darts he was starting to not be able to repel. This is why he'd wanted a wife in name only. He had little time for mooning over a woman. He also didn't want to end up like his parents, dead because their souls couldn't be together.

It was at that moment Cade realized it was already too late. That's why he'd let his walls fall the night before. He'd known it from the moment he'd seen Jacqui appear in the room as Damesha was giving birth. His soul had chosen Jacqui but he wouldn't allow himself to acknowledge it. Until now.

Cade sighed, alone in his office once more. What could he do? He was soul-mated and couldn't change that. He could control who knew it though. Leaving his office, he went to his suite of rooms on the same floor as Jacqui's. Just beside hers. Pressing his hand to the wall he wondered if she'd made it back yet. Leaning his forehead against the wall, he pictured her in her room, pale skin wrapped in black lace, her lips a deep slick red and felt his body respond.

He pressed his body to the wall now, wondering if she was in the room, waiting for him. Cade's blood surged in his veins and he wanted to press himself through the wall. He was so hard it was almost painful. He'd had other women in his bed, been in their beds, up against walls; he'd had his share of women, but none had ever gotten to him like this. Jacqui had a power he couldn't resist.

Lights playing over the ceiling let him know a car was in the driveway and he went over to the window to see who it was. Security would handle it but he wanted to know if it was her. Looking down from behind a curtain he saw her legs slide out of the car, their pale length shining in the darkness. He inhaled slowly as the rest of her followed.

Jacqui stood and turned, her torso leaning forward to speak to Kane and Damesha in the front seats. He wanted to bend her over his desk like that, her round tight bottom stretching the material of her pants before he pulled them off. His hand clenched in the curtain, his hardness even more painful.

He placed his hand over the rigid bulge, trying to ease it with a stroke or two but that only made it worse. He needed her, not his hand. He'd wait until she came up then go to her. She'd accept him and let him in, even if he had all but ignored her all day. She knew he was busy, that he had duties to tend.

Jacqui finally turned away from his brother and walked up the steps. She looked sad, shell-shocked. What had Evelyn told her to produce that look?

Cade watched her, anticipating having her in his arms once more when his phone buzzed.

"We need help, the back fifty are burning." A text from Jadrian.

Feeling like a prince trapped in his castle, Cade responded and then went down to his office to call in some of the other clan members. A fleeting memory of Jacqui's face in the moonlight stole Cade's breath but he reminded himself she knew who she'd married. He knew who he was as well, he reminded himself.

He'd made the right choice for his soul when he decided on her, that was obvious, but had he made the right choice for his family, for the people that depended on him when she distracted him so easily? Cade wasn't just the head of the family, he was the head of his clan, the laird, the king of his realm. Love could fuck all of it up.

Picking up the phone once again he started making phone calls and knew he wouldn't get much sleep tonight either. Memories of the night before and worry over his clan would war in his head as he fought to stay awake. He might have a moment of peace to relieve some of his tension, if he was quick about it.

Cade dismissed the idea, stretching out in his chair, pushing the seat back as he stretched his spine. He couldn't take a moment to pleasure himself knowing his clan members were out there fighting a fire, maybe fighting for their lives while he was trapped in his castle. Taking one more deep breath, Cade let his head fall back against the leather of the office chair. Just one moment of peace, that's all he needed, just one.

CADE JUMPED in the chair twenty minutes later, a loud knock at the door letting him know what had startled him out of his nap. Scrubbing at his face with large, well-used hands, Cade looked at the door. He had a feeling the knocker wasn't coming with good news.

He wanted to tell whoever it was to go away, leave him in peace, but this was the role Cade had accepted at far too young an age. This was what he'd been prepared for and would give his life up for. He supported well over two hundred people in his clan, he protected them and he served them. He kept the wolves at bay, literally. Especially werewolves.

Kane pushed through the door when Cade called

out, telling him to come in. Closing it quietly, Kane took a seat across from Cade and closed his eyes for a moment.

"I take it you were out with the fire patrol then?" Cade could smell the smoke in Kane's clothes and see black soot on his cheeks and neck. It looked to have been bad.

"Yes, I went out when I got back with Jacqui. Damesha wasn't happy about it but I had to do something. I couldn't sit there while it burned." Kane sounded exhausted but Cade liked this new Kane. Damesha had changed him, made him gentler, kinder, and easier to deal with because he wasn't always angry anymore. Cade appreciated her for that, if nothing else. Although he was coming to appreciate her for far more than that, Elspeth for one. Her devotion to the clan was another.

"Wives will never be happy when their men go out into danger. What did you learn?"

"It's all burned now, we'll have to buy hay for the winter from somewhere else. Or feed, whatever you want to feed the cattle, we'll have to buy it." The cattle were raised to feed the clan, to supplement their costs of living in such a small secluded area. Everyone in the town was either a shifter or the partner or child of a shifter.

"Our ancestors knew what they were doing, the clan

will provide the feed." Cade remembered the history he'd learned, a history that was kept from Damesha when she was researching the original Elspeth. Elspeth came into a town that didn't want her, or the other slaves, in their town. They mixed with the native populations, learning how to survive the frontier with them. The native clans slowly turned the new people into parts of their clan and Cade and his siblings were the result; a mixture of African, Native American, and white. Most of the other people in town were a similar combination of ancestry but some liked to pretend that mixture was so far back it was pointless to even consider now.

The former slaves had come together with the native populations to form a plan. Eventually, they bought out non-clan members or interbred with them. It was in everyone's best interests, now, to keep quiet about the clan's origins, who and what they were, and where they were exactly. In the name of staying hidden from the non-shifter world, it was forbidden to speak to outsiders about what they really were.

That secrecy sometimes caused members problems, like Kane when Cade refused to allow him to marry Damesha at first, but it was for the good of the clan. Cade had learned to be cold, hard but balanced as he'd grown into his role as clan leader. Sometimes he could bend those rules but until Kane had forced his hand with Damesha, he'd been unwilling to bend on allowing outsiders in. They were too much trouble and no matter how much people thought they were in love as soon as they started telling secrets, divorces could be deadly for his clan.

Rumors about shifters had abounded for generations. Hunted for sport in centuries past, the clans had gone into hiding, and now rumors led scientists in search of "specimens" to produce super-soldiers. The shifter world wanted to live only in peace as other humans did. Rumors were dangerous. Rumors had been spreading about Cade's sexuality lately, which was another problem. Homosexuals couldn't lead the clan because they couldn't produce children of their own bloodline. There had been talk lately of changing this rule but it hadn't been considered yet. That was part of the reason he'd married Jacqui, to dispel the rumors.

Cade had simply not planned on passing down his bloodline because he hadn't wanted to marry or have a family. A spouse and children would make him weak. He'd given in when the rumors started and found a wife that he thought would be perfect for the position. Jacqui was changing those ideas as she thawed his walls and he tried to thaw hers. Before he'd met her the clan encompassed his world and he devoted himself to his duties.

Now she was distracting him, taking away some of his devotion but that couldn't be a bad thing, could it? Clan leaders were expected to produce a family; he wasn't meant to devote his entire being to the clan was he?

Jacqui, with her icy shell and cool gaze had started a fire in him, a fire meant to melt the ice out of her heart. He'd wanted an ice queen but now he wanted to thaw her, to make her melt for him. That couldn't be bad because it was melting him too. Or was it a danger for the clan?

His overall devotion hadn't changed, he knew that, he'd still give his life for the clan but would it put Jacqui's life in danger? He knew he wouldn't, he'd give his last dying breath for either one. He just had to find a way to balance it all.

"So why are you here then, Kane? You could have called to tell me all of that." Cade looked at his brother with a probing gaze, he knew there was more to this visit.

"The rumors are still spreading. They're saying Jacqui's just your cover-up. I think the rumors are being spread by the Mungons. I don't think our people are doing anything more than repeating it." Kane looked angry for a moment but squashed it. Cade knew the anger was for him but anger wouldn't help anything, it would only make them sloppy.

"Some of our people are very close-minded people. I thought we'd come to a new age. I'll have to dispel them somehow."

"Getting her pregnant would work. It would shut them up for a little while anyway. And with an heir, well, you could do whatever you wanted to anyway." Cade knew Kane brought up a good point. As long as the child had his DNA, the gender didn't matter and neither did his sexual affairs after. Once a child was produced the rest didn't matter.

"You're right. I hadn't planned on a child so soon but... I guess plans are made to be changed." Cade smiled ruefully at his younger brother and watched him stand.

"I'll let you get to working on that and go see about producing another one myself. Damesha is insisting we wait but Elspeth needs siblings. And I sure do love that baby. I need more." Kane smiled happily and Cade watched his brother leaving, wondering at the change in his brother.

Damesha hadn't been the only thing that changed Kane, Elspeth had as well. Kane loved his daughter and doted on her already. Cade knew that could be a threat to him later in life, his love for his children, especially with the Mungons out to topple him and his family, but his clan was demanding a child. He'd give them one if

Jacqui agreed. For the good of the clan and maybe to save his own soul.

CADE WENT UP to Jacqui's room an hour later but she was asleep. Her right hand was tucked under her cheek and her lips were slightly parted. He had ideas about how to occupy her lips but the skin beneath her eyes looked bruised, her nose red, and her cheeks mottled. Had she been crying, was that why she looked like that?

Cade stepped back, his hand out to stroke down her hair but he stopped himself. Why had she been crying? Was it something Evelyn said or was it their night last night? Did she regret the night she'd spent in his arms?

He suspected she'd been a virgin but she hadn't said anything. That moment of resistance when he'd first entered her was something he'd never encountered before. Had she been a virgin and now regretted what they'd done?

She'd burned in his arms, burned with heat, not the burning sting of extreme cold. He'd never seen a woman respond so openly, so hungrily, surely that hadn't all been an act? If it was she was a damned good actress. Cade didn't believe that though, her body had responded to even his breath, whispered across her skin.

Such a response couldn't be faked. He'd felt her tight heat as she'd exploded and that couldn't have been faked either.

It must be something Evelyn said. What had the woman said to her? Cade settled on the sofa in her room to watch her sleep. He didn't want to leave her alone but it was obvious she needed to rest. He needed to think, to see if he could find a solution to what had made her cry. She was a part of the clan now, though she didn't know all of their secrets. That made her problems his and, in turn, his responsibility to resolve. He'd wait for her to wake, he'd just rest on the sofa for a little while until she stirred.

Leaning his head back against the soft pillows he was soon asleep, snoring slightly as the night passed on and his dreams took over his internal debate about whether he could afford to allow himself to love the woman or not.

8

———

Jacqui

Jacqui woke in the night, an odd sound stirring her from her dreams. It was a soft sound, like air escaping with a slight rumble behind it. Was it a snore? Rolling over she decided she didn't care and was almost asleep again when she realized that if the sound was a snore there was someone else in the room with her.

Fear froze her in place for a moment. Someone was in her room! She panicked, screaming internally at her muscles to run for the door but then sanity took over. Whoever it was they were asleep, which meant they weren't there to hurt her. And she was in Cade's house, anybody that managed to get in her room would have to belong here to get past the security that hid themselves in the shadows, always watchful but never speaking. The men and women of the security force had unsettled her at first but she'd grown used to them and stopped wondering why a man in the middle of a farm in Kansas would need a security force. They became almost a part of the furniture.

It must be Cade, she finally decided. Her muscles relaxed and she quietly pushed away her covers, walked over to see who was on the sofa.

Cade was there, his white shirt unbuttoned down to the middle of his chest, tie stripped away. His face was relaxed and his mouth was open slightly, his head to the side. Sleeping on his back he looked vulnerable, in need of a shave, and devilishly handsome. But could she let him into her heart?

Evelyn's news had been a blow; one she'd rather not have had. One minute she was a normal human being, well as normal as she could get, the next a witch who didn't have a clue how to use her powers. Evelyn had said something about an instructor but how would she explain that away to Cade? She sat on the oak table in front of the sofa and watched Cade sleep.

Her mother had told her secret and her father had used it to make himself rich, he'd used her until she had nothing left to give. Cade had riches she couldn't even imagine, he had power, and he'd done it all on his own. He wouldn't be the same as her father, would he? He wouldn't want to use her in that way.

Jacqui's thoughts had changed dramatically since she'd come to Kansas. She'd struggled to maintain her façade, her disinterest in the world. Last night had torn down walls she'd thought would never fall. She knew she could still display a level of reserve most people couldn't begin to fathom but could she hold herself back from Cade now? She knew she was falling for him but could she trust those instincts? Her mother had and she'd ended up in an early grave.

Jacqui reached out, wanting to touch the soft, silky black hair that shone in the moonlight. It looked like satin but she didn't get her hand near it before Cade was awake, his hand grasping at her to push it away.

"Sorry, I didn't mean to frighten you. Would you like to sleep in the bed instead of on this tiny sofa?" She had to smother a giggle because most of his legs were dangling over the other end. At well over six feet the tiny couch could barely contain him.

"I, um, oh, yes, please." Cade looked delightfully sleep-muddled and Jacqui wanted to hold him close to her heart and absorb some of the heat she knew he radiated. Passing a hand over his face he sat up. "Why do you keep it so cold in here all the time?"

"I hate being hot. You can always add more clothes but there comes a point where you just can't take anything more off to try to get cool. I like to sleep covered up too so I always keep it cold in my bedroom, at least." Having grown up in Florida, Jacqui knew a thing or two about heat, humidity and trying to stay cool.

"That makes sense." He still looked confused as he came to full awareness but then he seemed to remember where he was and his face took on a guilty look. "Sorry, I didn't mean to fall asleep."

"Not at all. I'm quite happy to find you in my room." She gave him an encouraging smile and he smiled back at her, reaching out for her hand.

"Shall we get under those covers you love so much then?" She stood with him as he got to his feet and walked to the bed.

"Indeed we shall but I think you'll be more comfortable out of those clothes." Her words were suggestive, urging him to strip down. Almost daring him.

Cade accepted the challenge and slowly began to unbutton the last remaining buttons on his shirt. He gave her a knowing smile as he pulled the shirt away from his taut abdomen and off his arms. Her left eyebrow twitched as she got a good look at him in the moonlight. Stunning.

His dark skin, so smooth to her touch, was meant for her lips and that flat stomach of his…oh my!

"Come here." She crooked her finger at him and he walked over, the belt to his trousers undone but not his buttons.

Jacqui slid her hand up his rigid length, pressing gently into him before she leaned forward, kissing his stomach.

She felt a shiver pass through him as he looked down at her wordlessly, his eyes on her face as she undid the button and pulled down the zipper. His pants slid down his legs, revealing bare skin. He hadn't been wearing any form of underwear! She liked that.

Jacqui took his erection in her hand, feeling the weight of him and the heat as her long fingers wrapped around him. She could only just get her nails to touch her palm. When he gasped she dragged her eyes from his rigid cock to see his eyes burning down into hers.

"Don't stop." His voice urged her on, to do more.

"Oh, I won't baby." She breathed the words against him and leaned forward again, dragging her tongue over the tip of him. It felt spongy, silky, but somehow hard. She wanted to taste all of him.

Jacqui moved again, her tongue moisturizing her lips before she let him slide into her wet depths. She heard him sigh and smiled as he went further, deeper, into her mouth.

"Were you a virgin last night, Jacqui?" The words stopped her, froze her in place with his cock in her mouth. She pulled away finally, wiping her wet lips with the back of her hand before she looked up at him again.

"What does it matter?" Her words were guarded, discouraging further questioning.

"I just thought you might have been and if you were, well, maybe you might want some instruction." He sounded as though he might run at any moment.

She didn't take his words as insulting, she took them with images of him sliding between her lips as he instructed her to open wider, suck harder.

"Then you might want to, whether I was or wasn't. I aim to please, after all."

"Alright." It was a simple way to say thank you, to display his relief at her not getting angry with him, of saying he wasn't going to force her to answer.

"How do you want me to hold your... cock, dear husband?" She used her best kitteny voice, a sultry voice that invited play.

"Just... oh... just like that." She tightened her grip on him once she took him in hand once more.

"And my lips?" She placed her lips on the tip of his organ, letting them rest there for a moment before darting out her tongue. She may have never done this before but she understood the art of teasing.

"Open." He strangled the words out as her tongue slid down his length and back up.

Jacqui opened her lips for him and he moved, thrusting into her mouth gently.

He paused as he slid in, realizing she couldn't open any further. "Suck."

She took his words as a command, but a gentle one, and did as instructed. Pulling her cheeks in, she sucked as she pulled away from him, letting her tongue drag underneath his length.

"Open." She placed her hand at the base, holding him steady as she opened once more. This time she opened her lips but only enough for him to slide between her teeth.

"Suck." His words were simple but oh so erotic as she watched his face tighten as she did as he told her to do.

She'd caught on and decided it was time to take matters into her own hands. Slowly at first, she started a rhythm that made him bury his fingers in her hair. She could feel him growing harder in her mouth and she sucked every time she came back up his length and figured out how to keep the friction going as she went down.

Cade's hips started to move in time with her head, his thrusts gentle so he wouldn't hurt her.

"Fuck, Jacqui." He strangled out the words, pulling away. She cried out as he pulled his cock from her mouth.

"But you didn't finish!" She'd wanted the whole experience! Doing this to him was really turning her on and she loved making him lose control. He'd taken that away from her.

"Later!" His words were a demand as he pulled her into a sitting position on the bed then pushed her back. "Open."

Her legs spread of their own will and Cade's tongue was soon in a place no tongue had ever explored before.

"Cade, stop! Oh god, wait no, oh fuck no don't stop!" He'd found her clit and her embarrassment and worries flew away as he sucked at her hard and fast, his tongue flicking at the button as she writhed against his face.

Jacqui felt her nipples tighten and tugged at the aching peaks, making the ache deeper, harsher, but not able to stop herself as Cade sucked at her clit. It felt too good to stop. She felt as though she were on fire but she didn't want the fire to go out, she wanted it to burn her to ashes, until she exploded into flames only Cade could put out.

Jacqui was just on the verge of something great,

holding her breath as the pressure built, as the fluttering started, when Cade reached inside of her, sliding into her wet depths with two fingers and finding just the right spot to make the world go dark as her body convulsed beneath him.

She heard a grunt of satisfaction, felt the hum of it on her mound, but didn't care as she inhaled sharply, her body bowing until she thought her back would break. She didn't care about that either because if this was how she was going to die it was the most perfect way ever. She rode the waves as his tongue lashed at her, propelling her further than she'd gone the night before.

For long minutes, pleasure surged through her. His tongue, his fingers never missing a beat as he sent her higher. Jacqui could no longer make words, she could only make noise as she tried to stay in the moment, fought with her own body to stay in that place of perfection where thought couldn't intrude.

With a sigh she finally came back to earth, slumping on the bed as Cade wiped his face and moved away.

"You can catch your breath but then I'm getting round two." He kissed her damp thighs, inhaling her scent before he came up beside her. He pulled her into his lap and stroked her hair as little aftershocks shook her. She could tell by the grin he wore as she peeked through her eyelids that he was pleased with himself. And so he should be.

Smug bastard. She couldn't stop the grin that stretched across her face as her brain finally engaged once more and she moved over him, stretching her body out to rest between his thighs.

"I think we need to take care of this." Her words stopped and spoke no more as she took him in her mouth, aiming to find out what all the fuss was about.

"Oh no, little one, I want that pussy of yours, I want to be buried up to my eyeballs in it. Come here." He pulled her up onto his lap and she moved with him, straddling his thighs so his hard length pressed into her.

She closed her eyes as she sank onto him, his rigidness invading her. A shudder passed through her when she could sink no more and she breathed deep as she let her body adjust to him. She knew he was big for the average male, but damn.

"Open." She knew he meant her eyes, so she opened her pale gaze to his. His dark eyes bored into hers and she gasped again, was that love there or just desire?

She pressed her lips to his as he sat up against the pillows, longing only for that place of abandon where the world didn't matter but she wanted to go there with him this time.

She found that if she moved just right her clit would

press into him and she began a rhythm that made her ears buzz. He seemed to enjoy it as his hands went to her hips, holding her steady as she rode him hard and fast. Their breathing came in quick gasps, mouths fused as they moved together, his up to her down. Together they sought that moment of release they both craved, and silently she found it.

Breaking away as she kept up her pace, Jacqui felt the pleasure surging through her once more, straight up her spine and into her brain. Cade followed, a low grunt his only sound as he surged inside of her, spilling himself in the wet confines of her heat.

Jacqui felt his explosions and moved to take him deeper, wanting every part of him to touch her, to stroke her insides. She rode him until her thighs ached and she couldn't move, her body too spent to move another inch. She sagged into him, her brain quiet for once in her life. The only thing she knew was the sound of his heartbeat.

She was almost asleep, not caring that her thighs and knees were on fire, she never wanted to move from this place of solace, her refuge. She didn't care how they'd started out, or that she barely knew him, this man was her savior. She knew the things she needed to know. Below that cold exterior that seemed to be harder than diamonds was a man of passion, a man who felt deeply, and wanted to please. She also knew he cared about his clan and would do anything for them. And she knew he wanted her. For now, that was enough.

"We have to move at some point, princess." He murmured the words sleepily into her ear.

"No, we don't. We can stay like this until we're fused together and will never come apart." She pouted against his shoulder, not even caring that he couldn't see her.

"I think we're about as fused as we're going to get." He gave a low chuckle that rumbled against her cheek.

"That may be but we don't have to move. Not yet." She gave a groan of protest as he rolled over to his side, taking her with him. Their bodies broke apart and she was no longer a part of him.

"Cheater! You're bigger than me. That's not fair." She pouted into her pillow this time.

"You need to sleep. We need to talk in the morning so don't go running off to have a bath, alright?" He kissed her neck as he cradled her, pulling her tight to him.

"I was a little, ahem, sore this morning." She said the words into his neck, still not wanting to face him.

"Ah, that explains it. Alright. We'll talk. In the morning. Go to sleep, princess. Unless you want another round." His tongue darted out to taste her neck and she was lost to him once more, her exhaustion vanishing as his hot lips moved over her skin. She would never be able to tell him no.

* * *

JACQUI WOKE up the next morning to find Cade had ordered in breakfast and had a table arranged with everything they'd need. She ran into the bathroom to wash her face after a kiss good morning and get herself decent then went out to join him. Tying the belt of her robe in place, she sat down and looked at the French toast. She loved how the chef cooked it here. She missed cooking though, it was one of the ways she could express herself back in Florida.

"Do you have a smaller home somewhere, Cade. A little place, maybe a cabin?" She was wondering if it was somewhere they could go to be together, just on their own, to act like the rest of the universe.

"I have a couple. One in Montana and one in Alberta." He looked at her quizzically.

"In Canada? Wow. That sounds nice, I'll have to dig out my passport. I'd like to see Montana as well." She took a bite and looked over at him. Something inside of her had shifted, softened, and she wanted to be more open with him than she was with most people.

"Maybe we can go when I can get away from this

place." He smiled at her and took a bite of his own biscuits slathered in sausage gravy.

"You have a really great chef, you know that?" She closed her eyes over the next bite. It was heaven.

"Rita is a great cook, I'll give her that. So, I don't know how to broach this with you so I'm just going to come straight out with it. How do you feel about getting pregnant?" He looked as if he was waiting for her to spit her food at him. A cross between terrified and resolute.

"Uh." She put her fork down, her brain spinning. "I think maybe we should have thought about that a few days ago, don't you?"

She might have been a virgin but she wasn't stupid. She knew how babies were made.

"You weren't on birth control?" He looked surprised.

"I didn't need it." Again she didn't say the words but he took her meaning. She'd been a virgin, there was no need. That's when the weight of the whole thing came down on him and he forgot about babies for a moment. She'd given him her virginity. He'd been her first, her one and only. Wow. She could see the thoughts going across his face and he didn't need to say a word, she knew exactly what he was thinking.

"No, of course not. Well." He looked lost and she felt sorry for him.

"I'm fine with having a baby if you are." She gave him

a reassuring pat on his hand and went back to eating. After spending so much time with Elspeth and knowing she was falling for Cade, she knew she wanted a child with him. "Is there any pressing reason?"

"There's a rumor I'm gay. I need to show that I'll pass on my DNA." Okay, she thought as she looked at his guilty looking face. Not a romantic reason but logical.

"Well then, we'd best get to it." She gave him a smile once more and went back to eating. Perhaps this wasn't the romantic morning she was hoping for but it beat the previous morning. With a happy sigh, Jacqui watched Cade as he finished his own breakfast.

None of this was going exactly to plan but when did life ever pay attention to the desires of humans? Fate had its own plan and it seemed to have gone far off-course of her own.

9

Cade

Cade watched Jacqui laughing as Elspeth's tiny fists reached for larger ones. Elspeth was three months old now, starting to focus and reach for things, her smile was actually a smile, whether doctors wanted to call it gas or not. Now that she was born her growth rate had slowed down to normal, according to the doctor's latest report, delivered by Damesha this morning. That was a good thing and something that got Cade to thinking.

They'd been making love every night, day, whenever the mood struck, for over a month now. Jacqui could be pregnant. If she was pregnant he'd have to explain why her pregnancy was going quickly. Possibly. He'd have to explain why she could communicate telepathically with their baby, possibly. And he'd have to explain about the shifter world. Probably. He hadn't thought about how to broach that yet.

Damesha and Kane were out shopping and Cade had asked them to leave Elspeth with them. Jacqui had picked up some pointers about caring for babies since she'd been here, she could change Elspeth in a flash, and Cade knew his way around babies so the couple had agreed. They'd been shocked but agreed.

Cade was just as surprised at the offer as they were, he hadn't planned on babysitting his niece today but his mind had made that decision. They had the baby on a pile of blankets on the floor of a sitting room and were playing with her. Cade used his phone to snap some photos and sent them to her phone. He knew she'd wanted to see just how relaxed and happy she looked. He couldn't believe this was the same ice queen that had walked in on the birth of the little girl she was now making baby noises to.

They'd both changed in dramatic ways and he was starting to see that as a good thing.

"You know your Aunt Jacqui is a miracle worker, Elspeth. Six months ago I didn't even want to know about you, now I'm figuring out the cost of building a stable for a pony in the back yard for you." Cade grinned down at the little girl while Jacqui swatted at his arms.

"Don't tell her you didn't want her. That's mean." She looked at him crossly but then leaned over to kiss him.

"I'm sure she can't understand me." But then again, she was a shifter, she might. She might shift too, which was why Cade knew he couldn't leave the baby alone with Jacqui. Babies couldn't control when or what they shifted into.

Elspeth had started shifting already, Kane had informed him. She was going to be a strong one.

Cade grinned at the baby and picked her up. Elspeth cooed and punched him in the nose. The tiny fist made him laugh and Cade gave her neck kisses until she giggled. He looked over at Jacqui and grinned.

"Yeah, I think I'll love this."

"I think I will too. It changes your life though. Even for the clan this is going to be a big change for both of us." She looked afraid for a moment, wondering if she'd be as big a failure at being a responsible parent as hers had been.

Cade knew what she was thinking, they'd talked about her childhood one night a few weeks ago and he knew she was worried she'd change after the baby came. He knew he'd be there for her no matter what.

"I think your mother really loved you, Jacqui. Your dad did a lot to abuse both of you and take advantage. You aren't going to experience that, I promise you." He had been shocked to learn about the witch part, mainly because he hadn't sensed it and still couldn't, but he was fine with it. He still hadn't told her his secret though. It was just too big to divulge without a really good reason and love, he was sorry to say, just wasn't enough of a reason.

Feeling guilty for his thoughts, Cade looked away as she took the baby.

"Any news yet?" He'd decided to change the subject. Jacqui hadn't wanted to invite anyone to train her and was still sporadically popping in coffee and treats but little more. She was happy the way she was and he wasn't going to force her hand.

"I'll hear back in a couple of hours. The urine test was positive but the doctor wants to be sure." She looked at him with hope in her eyes and gave him a tentative smile.

"Either way, we'll keep trying. I'd like to have a try now but we have company." He kissed his wife and smoothed a finger gently down Elspeth's downy head. Her hair was silky and black but her blue eyes just melted him.

A soft sound, almost a whisper but not came to Cade

as he looked at Elspeth. He looked over at Jacqui but she was cooing to the baby.

"What?" He thought the word in his mind and a giggle came into his head. Awareness came with it. His daughter.

"Oh." Cade stiffened with his sudden awareness of his child. He looked at Jacqui but she seemed unaware of it all. For now.

He'd be able to "hear" his baby in his mind until she was born, then the link could go or stay. It didn't always happen with non-shifter mothers, and didn't seem to have happened with Jacqui. It still might but until then he'd keep it to himself. He knew he had to tell her now, had been happy almost that he didn't know because non-shifter babies could have been possible, and in that case, he wouldn't have to tell her. But now, oh this changed it all. He'd have to tell her and he was terrified she'd run for the hills.

Even knowing she was a witch she didn't know that the rest of the myths were true as well. There really were werewolves, shifters, vampires, even things that had hidden themselves so well there were no longer human words for them. Things that hid in the darkness that used to have names but didn't anymore as antiquity shrouded them in dust. Things Cade hoped never to see brought back into the world.

"What do you want, a boy or a girl?" Jacqui was smiling at him and his heart melted but he felt guilty because he already knew what they were having. But, in his heart, it didn't matter. He was happy either way.

"Whatever we get, I'll love it." He looked away from her at that moment because they still hadn't said that word to each other, the L-word. It was too much of a chance still.

"So will I. I just want a healthy baby. It's more than I could have hoped for so it doesn't matter to me whether it's a girl or a boy."

For a moment a surreal fog settled over Cade. He knew this was all happening but he just couldn't believe it. Somehow he'd found this woman, his soul-mate, thousands of miles away and under totally unbelievable circumstances. He'd known when he'd seen her picture that she was the one, long before he'd read her file. He'd emailed her before he'd read it, in fact. He'd just taken a chance, an odd thing for him, and responded to her.

She'd looked perfect for the task at hand. He hadn't looked forward to a long, loveless marriage but she'd been beautiful, and something about her had drawn him. Behind that cold gaze had been a sadness he didn't understand. But then, she was looking for a mail-order husband, something had to be off. He'd expected a lesbian-in-hiding or a woman with mental problems maybe but she'd checked out on that front. He'd learned why she wanted an arranged marriage when she told him about her parents and that night, the night when she opened all of her doors to him, he'd finally admitted he loved her to himself.

He'd made the right choice then and he hoped he was making the right choice now by delaying the telling of his secret. Her phone rang and with a shaky hand, she answered it. He waited, knowing what the answer was but he was surprised by her look of disappointment. She looked so sad!

Jacqui turned the phone off and gave him a sad smile. "We keep trying I guess."

"But…" He stopped himself. He couldn't explain it to her without revealing how he knew. "You haven't had a period."

"They can change, sometimes it happens. Stress, who knows?" She patted his arm and gave him Elspeth. "I think I need to lie down, Cade. You can bring her up if you want to but I just, I need to lie down."

"It'll be alright, princess. I promise you." He hugged her gently with one arm and watched her walk away. He'd let her have some time while he tried to figure out what was going on. "We're calling that doctor back, Elspeth. His test is wrong."

Cade's name carried weight in town and when he

called the doctor's office the receptionist put him through. The doctor must have been with another patient because he was breathless when he answered the phone.

"What can I do for you, Cade?" The man sounded nervous. So he should be.

"Why did you tell her she's not pregnant when she is? I can sense the baby." Cade hadn't wanted to divulge that information but it was necessary to explain to the doctor how he knew she was.

"That's impossible, Cade. Unless she's a witch these tests are very accurate. That would be the only way."

Cade clammed up at that point, there was no need for him to tell the clan Jacqui's secret through the doctor. "Well, she's not a witch. But she is pregnant so I guess this is a fluke. You're going to call her right back, right now, and tell her she is pregnant. Understand me?"

Cade's voice held just enough menace that Cade heard him telling the receptionist to get Jacqui on the other line right away. Cade stayed on long enough to hear the doctor explain there must have been some mistake and to hear Jacqui running down the stairs before he hung up. He caught her just as she threw herself at him, careful of Elspeth in his other arm.

"They called back, the test was positive after all! We're having a baby!" She was all but jumping up and down and Cade watched her with a heart brimming with joy of his own.

"We'll start clearing a room for the nursery right away. We'll get the builders in at the same time we get them in for Elspeth's pony's barn. That was a tough sentence to say. But yes, a nursery, a barn, a pony. Oh I need to sit down." For a moment Cade felt overwhelmed.

He hadn't really wanted a child of his own but from the moment he sensed her presence, he'd loved the baby growing inside of Jacqui. He wanted her and the joy she was going to bring to their family. He wanted this stupid war over and he wanted his wife to know everything. Including that he loved her.

"Jacqui, I know this might be an awkward time to mention it but I want you to know something." He looked over at her as she sat on the couch, the words already in his eyes. "This might not be the life we had planned, and it's certainly not what we were expecting to get but fate has brought us together. We're meant for each other. You're my reason for breathing, more and more every day and I just, well I just couldn't imagine life without you in it, princess. I love you."

Jacqui's eyes welled up and she leaned over to kiss him, Elspeth giggling happily between them. "I love you, Cade. This hasn't been easy but you've made it seem like it is. It is so easy to love you. So wonderful to love you. I couldn't have imagined this life but now I don't want anything else, just you, our baby, and to be with you."

They were cuddled up on the couch, Elspeth asleep in Jacqui's arms when Damesha and Kane came in.

"Now that is a picture moment! Hold still you two!" Damesha gave a wide grin as she held her phone up to snap a picture of the happy aunt and uncle with their niece. That one was going to be printed and framed.

Cade gave an embarrassed smile and hugged Jacqui closer. He wasn't ashamed to admit he loved his wife but it was so new, private even, that he felt a little embarrassed to let others see it. Old habits can sometimes die hard and allowing people to see a softer side of him was going to take some getting used to.

Jacqui gave a wide smile of her own and looked at Damesha happily. They'd decided to let the family know but were going to ask that it be kept a secret for a while longer, just until Jacqui was comfortable letting others know. For Cade's part, it was something to worry over, an Alexander baby was something to be bargained over if the baby disappeared. Especially the leader's baby.

A pregnant wife also made Cade weak in the eyes of his enemies. He had something he valued and would act to protect at all costs. Something else to bargain over.

With a sigh, he shook his head in agreement when Jacqui looked at him expectantly.

"We have news." Her grin was infectious but for the first time, Cade noticed how anxious and tense Kane seemed. Damesha didn't exactly appear to be her normal self either, despite her smile. There was a tenseness around her eyes.

"What's up?" Cade was instantly on alert. Damesha was psychic after all.

"I'd like to speak to you privately." Kane had gone all formal and that wasn't a good sign. Even worse, he wanted to speak privately. This was about Jacqui then.

"Wait a minute princess, let me see what's up, then we'll tell them, alright?" Cade leaned over to kiss her gently before he left with Kane. Yes, he'd allowed others to see him kiss his wife, this really was a brand new world.

"What's up?" Cade asked as soon as the door closed behind Kane once they reached his office.

"The Mungons are going to try to kidnap Jacqui." Kane didn't have to explain how he knew that.

"Did Damesha see when or how?" Cade's chest tightened at the news and he wanted to pound someone's face in. They would not touch his wife.

"No, but soon I'd guess. She noticed the leaves had turned. They'll be turning any day now." Cade was always impressed with Damesha's observational skills.

"Alright." Cade sat at his desk, his head nodding but he wasn't sure at what. "Increase security, nobody gets in here without a full check and scan, even you and our brothers. I'm going to take Jacqui away for a few days."

He'd made the decision in the moment but he had a thought. "She was kidnapped from here right?"

"Yes, from her room. They can't do that if you aren't here. Good plan. Go to one of the unlisted houses." They had houses across the globe, in a variety of locations. "Don't tell me which but let me know when you get there. I'll let the staff know to get some clothes packed. You get your wife."

"She's pregnant, Kane. We can't let them put their hands on her." Cade looked at his brother with pain in his eyes, a pain Kane understood. Kane clasped his brother's hand and squeezed it.

"We won't let that happen, brother. We'll keep her safe." They gave each other a deep look before breaking apart, their words a vow.

"Oh good, you're both back, so we have news..." Jacqui's words broke off as Cade came back into the room. "What's wrong?"

"We have to go, now. Kane, forget the clothes, we'll get something on the road. I'll take the Hummer, it's loaded." By that he meant with money, a registered handgun, and fuel. It was always kept on standby.

"But Cade…" Jacqui looked terrified for a moment then her wall came down. He knew she understood and turned off her fear. "Lead the way."

"I'll call you from a payphone, Kane, later." He sent a look to his brother and took his wife's hand. It was going to be a long day but it would keep them safe. All three of them.

10

Jacqui

Jacqui had no idea where they were going or why but she knew that she was going to get answers one way or another. She let Cade drive in peace for now, the white-knuckled grip he had on the steering wheel told her to wait, but later there'd better be some answers. To a lot of her questions.

Cade drove for two hours before his hands relaxed on the steering wheel. Jacqui had her phone on, reading a book, when she heard him sigh and looked over at him.

"Better?" She didn't sound accusatory, just concerned.

"A little bit, yes. I'm sorry, princess." He shot her a look that said he really was.

"Where are we going?"

"I think to Arkansas. At least for tonight. We'll see how it goes."

"Do you think we could stop soon? My bladder might explode if we don't and we need to eat."

"Yeah, babe, if you'd said earlier I'd have stopped." He looked at her apologetically.

"I think you needed to drive for a while first. That looks fine, we can get some gas, some food, and get back on the road."

She was pointing at a sign advertising one of those all-in-one places. It had a burger joint, which was fine with both but neither had been to one in years. She hadn't eaten at one since Evelyn found her. She wasn't above eating at one but she'd just never missed that kind of food. Now, though, the thought of salty fries was a temptation that grew in her mind the closer they got. She told Cade what she wanted as she headed for a restroom and he filled up the tank.

She found him in the restaurant, sitting at a table with their food.

"That was fast!" She slid across from him and sipped at the clear soda he'd got for her.

"Yeah, most of it was already cooked so don't expect much. It's probably been sitting under lights for an hour." He gave her an amused look as she bit into her hamburger.

"No! Oh my god, that is so good!" Her face was a picture he'd only ever seen in their private moments. He couldn't believe it but it was true.

"This is probably the best burger of my life! And oh, I'm going to need more fries. Please, Cade, get me some more?" She didn't even look shocked at her own behavior, she just looked at him with a pleading look.

"It must be the baby or you got a fresher burger than I did. Mine tastes like cardboard."

She looked at him confused for a moment then realization, and blushing, dawned. "I'm sorry, honey. Yeah, it must be the baby. I don't each much meat anymore and I guess maybe it likes having some protein other than beans and tofu?"

She wasn't strictly vegetarian but meat was something she'd moved away from long ago. She still ate it sometimes but it wasn't necessary for her to keep breathing. Maybe the baby had needed it?

They laughed as she wolfed down another burger, two more orders of fries and a milkshake before they left. She could barely move but she finally felt satisfied as they walked out to the Hummer, hand in hand. She was smiling, telling him she thought she might be able to cram in a hot fudge sundae when he took out a phone. It was an old cheap cell phone. He pressed some buttons, held it to his ear, then took out the battery and threw it in the trash. That sobered her up.

This wasn't just a holiday drive to a park, this was serious and she still didn't know what was happening.

"I'm going to keep quiet for now, let you drive, but when we get wherever it is we're going you're going to talk to me, Cade, and you're going to tell me exactly what is going on and what that phone business, what this running away business is about." She crossed her arms and stared out of the window. She knew she looked petulant but didn't care.

She'd known from the beginning that this wasn't a normal marriage but they were running away. It didn't make sense that a simple farmer, well a super-rich farmer, and head of a large family should be running away unless they were running from something bad. The law? Some kind of organized crime farm mafia? She had no idea but she did know that this wasn't going to cut it.

"Babe?" Cade looked over at her with a guilty look.

"Yes?" She'd glanced at him then turned her face away.

"I need you to toss your phone. It can be tracked."

"You need me to what? I know you have a lot of money Cade but there's, this phone was, oh you can't be serious? My life is on this phone!" She clutched it to her chest, cradling it.

"I'm afraid I am. We can find a post office and you can mail it back to the house if you want but we can't keep it on us. We need to ditch it before we get to Arkansas."

For a moment she thought her head would explode, but she brought down a wall. "Find a post office, I simply can't throw it away. It has too much on it to just throw away."

She sounded like the old Jacqui and for a moment she felt a sting in her heart. Then she pulled up another wall and pushed the stinging sensation down. He'd better have a very good explanation for all of this. A very damned good one.

They found a small post office off the highway and soon had her phone going back to their house. She wanted to cry as she left the post office but wouldn't let herself. She didn't cry. Period. Not when she was awake anyway.

They drove for two more hours and Cade pulled up to a mall with a department store inside. He left her with a stack of money and told her he'd be back in a few, that she needed to find enough clothes and toiletries for a week, and to meet him at the water fountain in twenty minutes. She was so upset she didn't ask where he was going but she did wonder why he'd leave her if it was such a dangerous time for them. She knew he must feel they were safe now and went into the nearest clothing store.

She came out with several bags and found him at the fountain, a few bags of his own in his hand. She saw he had a bag with a few boxes of shoes in it and wished she'd remembered to buy some of her own. All she had were the trainers she had on. She sighed and thought it was a problem for another day and went with him into another department store, looking for food.

They needed two buggies by the time they were done, one for the clothes and one for the household items and food they bought. She'd never purchased so much stuff at one time. She hadn't been poor over the last few years but this was something she'd never done before. She almost felt embarrassed.

Jacqui pushed the cart with the clothes while Cade pushed the heavier one. It was going to be a long night of unpacking, putting stuff away, and organizing. Cade stopped at another place before they got to the car, bringing four large pizzas with him.

"I got the meat specials since you seem to be on a

meat kick for the moment." He gave her a grin but she just glared at him, still upset with him despite the joy the smell of the pizzas brought her. It was hard to stay mad at a man that tried to fulfill your every desire. Even ones you didn't realize you had.

They pulled onto a secluded dirt road, heading deep into the woods. Jacqui thought it must have been miles before they reached a small cabin with a lake glittering behind it in the moonlight.

"Wow." She breathed as she saw the place. A real life cabin in the woods. But then she remembered she was mad at him and clammed up.

Cade didn't say anything other than to guide her into the house with a flashlight and the keys. She turned on the light, slid the key into the lock, and opened the door. It was done up in a country style, rather than a hunting style, and she felt some relief over that. It had obviously seen a woman's touch and there wasn't much that would consume electricity other than a television, the fridge in the kitchen, and the lights. Even the cooking range was wood and wouldn't use a bit of electricity.

"Oh my, I've never cooked on one of those before." She bit her lip with worry as she saw Cade come in behind her.

"You sit down and eat, I'm going to start bringing this stuff in and putting it away." He gave her a hopeful smile but she just raised her left eyebrow and turned away, opening a pizza box.

She wasn't sure how it was possible, but by the time Cade sat down and opened his own box, Jacqui had eaten two entire large pizzas stacked with meat and cheese. She looked at him guiltily but then turned her head. Nope, still mad at him.

She wished Annie were there to pet while she curled up in bed. The dog had become a companion as time had gone on. Jacqui knew Annie was devoted to Damesha, but she wanted to stroke the dog's long red ears until she was calm again. Annie always knew when something was wrong and it didn't matter who they were, if they'd pet her she'd love on them. She wanted a dog like Annie.

"Um, Jacqui, what did you do?" Cade's voice broke into her reverie and she saw that he was looking at the floor beneath the small table they were sat at. An old table made from rough-hewn pine the table fit in with the rest of the rustic décor.

She didn't see anything. Not until a little red tail came wagging from under Cade's chair. A little red tail attached to a fat wiggling bottom. Oh dear.

"I was thinking about Annie. You don't think?" She paused standing to look under the chair. Sure enough, a small puppy almost identical to Annie was under the table. Instead of the white heart shaped line between Annie's eyes, however, there was a black line.

"Oh my. How are we going to explain this? What are we going to feed her?" Jacqui did a quick check. "Yep, she's a her."

"Leftover pizza?" Cade looked heartbroken for a moment and Jacqui wasn't sure why.

"I'm sorry, Cade. But I have her now…"

"It's not that, princess. It's just, well, here." He handed her a bag he hadn't touched since bringing it in and looked crestfallen. "It's not going to compare to you blinking yourself up a puppy though, is it? You're going to be mad at me forever now!"

Well, he'd noted her anger then. That was a good thing. And he'd bought her a present! She sat with the puppy in her lap, the little almost copy-cat dog wiggling around, wanting to love on Jacqui as she opened the bag. She saw the logo for the phone she'd just shipped back to the house and her eyes flew to Cade's.

"You got me the new one? But it's a fortune!" She pulled the box out and between trying to hold onto the puppy now licking her face and opening the box she somehow managed to knock one of the pizzas off of the table. The puppy jumped down and started chowing down on the pizza so Jacqui let her.

"I know you need your phone. This one's not registered to a name so it'll be fine. I had the salesperson set it up for you. You can't use any of your accounts yet but you can at least find some books to read and play movies and stuff." Cade looked down at his hands and waited for her to respond.

Jacqui couldn't decide which was more exciting, the puppy or the phone and wanted to reach for the puppy but she saw Cade's eyes and knew she needed to make an effort for him. She was still upset, but he'd tried and that mattered. She went to him, sitting in his lap as she wrapped her arms around his neck.

"You didn't have to do that, honey. I appreciate it, I really do. And when we get home I can migrate all my stuff to this one. But first, we have some talking to do. Grab one of those beers for yourself, a pair of pajamas, and let's go check out that bathroom. I'll figure out somewhere for the puppy to sleep tonight." They kissed and Jacqui knew her life was about to change again but didn't mind this time. Now she'd have some answers.

She went into the bathroom to find a bathtub, almost the exact same tub as the one in her room. That figures, she thought, as she started to fill the tub with hot water. It was an awesome tub, after all.

They both got in once it was full and relaxed for the first time in hours, the puppy asleep on a towel in the corner.

"Cade, it's time. You have to tell me what's going on. I can't live like this, with not knowing." He'd begun to wash her hair and she wanted to let him go on but couldn't stand it anymore.

"Let me rinse your hair." He used a plastic cup to rinse her hair, taking far longer than he needed to.

"Stop stalling, buddy!" she said, moving to the other end of the tub to face him.

He sighed and looked away, his mouth crooking to one side as he thought. He finally came to a decision and started to speak.

"I guess blunt and to the point is always the best way, isn't it? My family and I, my brothers, the people in town, my clan, all of us except a few, are shifters."

She looked at him with her brows knitted together. She knew that word but she'd forgotten about it.

"What does that mean?" Her voice was snappy but she didn't mean it to be.

"Well, we can shapeshift into any animal we want to." He watched her closely, waiting for her to bolt or scream that he was insane.

"Pull the other one while you're at it." She held her right leg out to him.

"I'm not joking. Even Elspeth is."

She wasn't buying it. "Right…" She waved her hand in a 'carry on' fashion.

"Jacqui, you're a witch and you still don't believe me?" He sounded astonished and moved away from her.

"You can't really expect me to! I mean, a shifter? Okay, a little twitchy magic is one thing but shifters? That's just, well, unbelievable…" Before she could finish Cade disappeared and a black crow stood on the end of the tub where he'd been.

Jacqui stared at the silky black bird as it squawked at her and ruffled his feathers before hopping along the edge to come and stare into her eyes. Those were Cade's eyes. Smaller and rounder but definitely Cade's. Her left eyebrow rose as the bird hopped onto her hand and bowed down.

"Shit! You can turn into a crow?" Jacqui knew it was a silly response but it's what came out, she couldn't stop it.

Before she could blink Cade was back in the tub, only sitting on the edge this time.

"Okay, that's a huge secret. Huge. But what do you do?" She looked at him and she could see he was relieved that she was still sitting there and not screaming. She felt a small sense of pride that she wasn't but she'd seen it herself. There was no denying it.

"What do you mean, what do we do?" Cade looked confused as he sat back in the hot water now speckled with bubbles from her shampoo.

"Well, vampires suck blood, werewolves eat people or something, there's never one "reason" for werewolves is there, or explanation of exactly what they are, mummies kill people seeking revenge. What do shifters do?" She watched him as she spoke, waiting to see his reaction. She hadn't meant it to sound insulting but he might have taken it that way.

"Well, we protect more than anything. A long time ago we protected the tribes, we kept them safe from other tribes, from wild animals, things like that. Now, well, we do the same thing but now most of us that remain are shifters." He took her in his arms as she moved back towards him.

"Alright. So you're part of the Native American culture?" She settled into his chest, needing his touch to reassure her.

"Yes, we're part of that. We've taken on a lot of other cultures over the years, now we're a mix of many races and cultures. But we still hold onto our beginnings in many ways. Oh, I was a raven by the way, not a crow." He chuckled at the end, hugging her tightly. It was going to be alright, between them at least. Until she realized their kid might be a shifter. That might change her mind.

"I'm not an ornithologist. So why are we running, Cade? I might not feel so helpless if I know what I'm running from." She realized then her walls had fallen again, she had admitted how helpless she'd felt all day.

Cade pulled her close once more, toe on the taps to reheat the water, and started to explain his life to her. His entire life.

11

———

Cade

Cade watched as Jacqui prepared a dinner of roasted chicken and vegetables on the old wood cook stove as though she'd always used one. He'd learned she was highly adaptable over the last eight days and that there was little that daunted her. She potty-trained her new puppy and had already taught her to sit and was making headway with getting her to sleep in her own bed, not theirs. Cade didn't think that was going to take but he was fine with having the puppy at their feet.

Jacqui was even chopping the stacked wood outside into smaller pieces to fit into the stove's firebox all on her own now. He was glad to see the delicate ice queen had turned into a fiery provider, he knew she was strong enough to deal with what was coming.

Not necessarily a domestic goddess, he knew she'd emasculate him for that, she'd grown into a woman that loved to cook and clean, but also loved being pampered. That wasn't to say he sat around doing nothing all day, he did his fair share of cutting wood, cleaning and cooking as well. It was just nice to see that she was, well, human. And the way she smiled now, Cade closed his eyes and inhaled deeply.

It was probably a matter of how they both smiled now. He'd never been so far away from his clan for so long but he enjoyed the peace, the tranquility of not always being "on". He'd started to feel like a machine, a tool to be used and being in the cabin with Jacqui had changed that. He was happy, he realized, something he'd never really thought about before. He'd not felt that way since the death of his parents and Jacqui had brought it back to his life.

"You're beautiful, you know that?" Cade watched as she pulled the chicken out of the oven and set it on the top of the stove to rest. Her puppy, newly named Mary, followed her in the hopes of a dropped morsel.

"It's your fault. Pregnancy glows and all that stuff. I had no idea I'd sweat so much!" She wiped her forehead with a towel and turned to him, a handkerchief tied around her hair to keep it out of her face. Her eyes were clear, bright, and smiling.

"God, how I love you!" She melted into his lap and kissed him as he growled out his pleasure at having her in his arms. "Can't we skip dinner? I bet this table is sturdy enough to take what I have in mind."

"No! Your daughter wants feeding and so do I. Let me up!" She giggled as his tongue began a long stroke up her neck and melted deeper into his arms. "Oh don't stop."

"I thought you wanted feeding?" He murmured against her neck, his lips teasing her sensitive skin.

"Oh, I do." She said in a low sultry voice that had him surging into her with his hips.

"Nope, you need food right now, let's eat." She gave him a baleful stare but stood up. Mary, devoted to the woman of her dreams, followed along, licking a bare leg in adoration.

Jacqui laughed and petted the puppy before dropping down a piece of chicken for the dog. "You're as greedy as me!"

Together they plated up the food and sat down to eat. They were just emptying their plates when Jacqui looked up at Cade guiltily.

"I thought that would be enough. I guess we'll have to have that chocolate pie now." Jacqui was denying herself little with the pregnancy, a firm believer in eating what your body craves.

"I'll get it out. Shall I just bring two spoons?" He was serious and that made her laugh. He smiled with her, knowing that yet again this was their normal now. Life kept changing lately but it was all for the better. For the moment anyway.

"I think that would be wise. I can feel her moving around in there every time I think about that pie." Jacqui's pregnancy was advancing as quickly as Damesha's had, and he'd told her about his connection with their baby. He knew she was disappointed that she didn't seem to have it so he shared with her all he knew about the baby so far.

"So what was that name you wanted to give her again?" He'd brought the silverware and was busy digging into the pie with her.

"Stella Amanda Alexander." Jacqui stopped eating long enough to say the name then went right back to eating.

"Why Stella?" He gave her a quizzical look.

"I just like it." Back to eating. He smiled as he watched her. She really loved eating now but it wasn't making her gain weight so he knew she needed it.

"I was thinking I'd like to name her Anastasia." He spoke tentatively, unsure of how she'd respond to his offer of a name. Men weren't supposed to think of girl names and such were they?

"Oh, I do like that! How about Anastasia Stella Alexander?" She looked at him happily. He should have known she wouldn't laugh at him.

"That works for me. That really does." He realized they had a name for their daughter now and suddenly she became even more real. She had a name, a presence, and would soon be here. He was stunned by the realization. His daughter was real!

"Stunning isn't it? We're having a baby!" Jacqui's intuitive interpretation of his thoughts had stopped shocking him and had become normal to him now.

"It is. Wow. Anastasia. Just, wow."

They both stopped as a deep vibration started to make the whole house buzz. At least it seemed like it until they realized it was Jacqui's new phone. Who could be calling them? She looked to Cade for an answer but he knew who it was.

"Kane. He's the only one that has the number. Unless it's a wrong number. Or a telemarketer." He went and found the phone between the cushions of the couch. Obviously, this one wasn't as important as the phone she'd sent back to the house in Kansas.

"Hello?" He put the phone on speaker as he connected, knowing Jacqui had followed him in. She was going to be a part of everything now, she knew the secrets, she'd know them all.

"Cade, they have Damesha. We need you." Kane sounded distraught and angry. On the verge of doing something very stupid, Cade could tell.

"I'll be there shortly brother, send the helicopter." Cade looked over at Jacqui in dismay. She looked terrified, he knew she loved Damesha.

"We're on the way already, we should be there in an hour. Cade, don't delay, please. I'll go in by myself if I have to." Kane's voice, so like Cade's, shook as he spoke.

"I understand the bond now, Kane, I do. I know it won't be long before you start to feel the separation. How far is she?" Cade had explained to Jacqui that the further the distance, the longer the separation was, the quicker the damage was done to the spirit-bound partners. The same would happen to them if they were separated.

"She's far, Cade, very far. And getting further. It's not so bad now that I'm in the air, I think we must be getting closer. I think we're heading to Texas. I'll know when they stop moving." Kane's voice was strained and Cade knew it was pain.

"Alright, where's Elspeth?" Cade gestured to Jacqui to get ready, he wasn't leaving her on her own.

"Jadrian and Jacob are taking her to Montana." Kane

coughed, a dry sound that made Cade frown. He didn't have long.

"Good. She'll be safe there with them." The Montana house was underground and impenetrable once the hatch was closed, even from other magicals.

"I know. I'm going to cut this off now. I'll see you in a bit. Be ready." Cade knew Kane would only allow the helicopter to land long enough to pick them up before taking off again. He had to, he didn't have long before his body started to shut down.

That's part of the reason it took his parents so long to wither and die. They weren't separated by a great distance. A few acres really, nothing more, but enough to cause the withering.

Cade and Jacqui flew through the house, closing and locking everything. They were standing outside in the clearest spot for landing when the helicopter came down, hooded sweatshirts over t-shirts against the cooling night air. Mary was wrapped in a blanket, her little head bobbing around happily as she watched what was going on. She ducked into the blanket when the helicopter came down and shivered in Jacqui's arms. They ran for the doors as the machine came down and Cade had barely closed the door when Kane signaled the pilot to go back up.

"Where are we going?" Cade asked as he put on headphones so he could hear his brother.

"Louisiana, down in the bayou around Houma. I'll know more once we get there." Cade's eyebrows rose for a moment. Back to Louisiana then.

He'd had to fill his days with endless meetings while on his honeymoon to distract himself from the beautiful wife he thought wouldn't accept his advances. If only he knew then what he knew now.

Cade glanced over to see Jacqui in ice queen mode once more. Not because of him but because he knew that she was preparing to do whatever it took to get Damesha back. The only sign of his loving wife was the way she stroked Mary to calm her as the helicopter flew through the air.

"How did they get her, Kane?" Cade was trying to distract his brother, the brother that was going to chew his own fingers off if he kept gnawing at them like that.

"They waited until we were in bed. They've been tormenting her for ages and we thought it was the clan. They stand out there, calling to her with different animal sounds. She thought she was crazy for a long time. I guess they learned our patterns then." Kane sighed, staring out of the glass to his left.

"No, that wasn't anything the clan was doing. I wish I'd known." Cade knew why Kane hadn't told him, he'd been a dick to his brother and he knew it. He understood that now. "I'm sorry."

"You were doing what you thought was best for the clan, Cade. I know that." Kane sighed again.

"Still, I should have been a little more understanding. We'll get her back, try not to worry." Cade patted his brother from his seat behind him.

The rest of the flight was spent making plans, plans that saw Jacqui right at Cade's side. He was *not* letting her out of his sight. He knew in movies they always told the woman to stay put but he always thought that was stupid. Leaving her would do nothing but distract him as he worried over what he couldn't see. No, his wife would be right by his side.

Jacqui stayed quiet, listening to the men plan, but knew she was involved. Cade watched her and saw a fierce resolution come over her. Yes, she'd be an asset. Smart, observant, and a quick thinker, Jacqui would not be a hindrance.

They soon landed in a town just outside of Houma, a car was waiting for them. Jacqui handed Mary over to the man waiting with the keys after Cade assured her the man would take her to safety. They piled into the car and Cade followed Kane's directions. They headed down a dirt road and stopped as lights came into view. Stashing the car on the side of the road, they stalked up to the house quietly. Cade looked down at Jacqui's footwear and knew her choice of trainers was a good one.

Things went all to Hell the moment they got near a window and heard a nasty male voice demanding answers from a whimpering Damesha. When Jacqui heard flesh smacking flesh, she went ballistic. Cade tried to stop her but with a dropped jaw and round eyes all he and Kane could do was watch as she strode up the front steps, kicked in the door, and started doing…something with her hands. Men flew against walls, women screamed, and Cade and Kane finally moved, guns suddenly in their hands as they stalked in behind the witch that had just found her powers.

"Where is she?" Cade saw Jacqui's eyes had a dark green glow to them as she held her hands aloft. Looking up he saw a fat, scruffy man with a long dark beard in the air, a wet spot in the front of his pants.

The man couldn't speak and his face was turning red but his eyes moved to a wall to his left. Going to the wall, Kane kicked it in, not caring that there was a release for the hidden door somewhere. The man fell to the floor unconscious, and Cade followed Kane into the room.

A blast of cold flew past Cade and he heard a male scream as the sound of an impact came from the room.

The twin of the other man, this one was trying to scream as Jacqui's energy held him against the ceiling. Kane flew to Damesha, releasing her from the rope bonds holding her in the chair.

Jacqui's demeanor was cold, heartless, and Cade knew if he didn't do something soon she'd kill every single person in the house she didn't love. Stunned at his wife's sudden power, he walked up to her carefully.

"We need to question these people, honey. Let him down. Knock him out if you want to but let him down without killing him, please." Cade stroked her cheek, her eyes still glowing, as she let the man down.

With a shake of her head, the glowing stopped and she looked at her husband.

"Oh my." Her eyes were round, shocked, but full of glee. "I'm sorry. That wasn't the plan at all was it?"

"No, but it definitely worked. Well done." He took her hand as they walked around the house, pulling people into the middle. Jacqui somehow pinned them all down without touching them as Cade called in help from an allied clan.

"I'm taking her to a hotel. I'll call you later." Kane came in with Damesha in his arms, she hid her face as they came into the light. Jacqui growled, looking back at the men.

She knew which one had done it, twin or no twin,

and he'd get the worst of it if he didn't tell Cade whatever he wanted to know.

"What's going to happen to them? Once we're done with them?" She turned to Cade as Kane left.

"If you leave anything sizeable enough they'll go before the magical court. The court will decide whether they continue to exist or not. They can't move, right?" Cade began to walk around the large house.

There were no leaders here and that confused him, but there were a lot of papers. Plans he saw. Plans for destroying the magicals in America in order to take over.

"Look at this. They plan to take over the country and turn Europe into a V-Farm." Cade held a paper out to Jacqui.

"What's a V-Farm?" She took the paper studying it.

"Some idea they've come up with. They plan to enslave the humans of America, make them work for the vampire blood." He said the words as if they'd make sense to Jacqui.

"Pardon? Humans can drink vampire blood without, you know, becoming a vampire?" She looked really confused.

"Oh yes, you only turn when it's done ritualistically. Otherwise, the whole world would be full of them. No, humans can and do consume vampire blood. It's very addictive and can make you magical for a short while if you can get past the euphoria it causes." Cade sounded like he was disgusted.

"That's just gross. Ew! Just ew! And they want to get their humans addicted to this to enslave them? The ones they allow to live?" Jacqui was eyeing the group of werewolves and shifters once more.

"Yes, the Mungon's seem to have formed an alliance with the werewolves. This isn't good. And it's not over yet. Shit." Cade scrubbed at his face as he looked at his wife. "But we have you. We're going to have to go before the magical court. Ask for help with this. Form alliances. Damnit, I should have done all of this already but I had no idea it was this bad. I thought they just wanted to destroy my clan."

"Why your clan?" Jacqui looked as though she was deciding which one was going to get their nails pulled out first as she spoke to her husband. Cade pulled her away from them as members of the ally clan showed up.

"My clan is the most powerful and oldest in the world. If they take us down the whole thing crumbles." He shook hands with the woman, a very beautiful woman with almost translucent white skin, eyes as blue as the sky, and hair the color of the flames he so loved to watch. Very beautiful indeed.

"We can't allow that to happen." Even Jacqui turned

as the woman spoke, her allure prickling into Jacqui's brain.

"Oh my." Jacqui's new favorite catch phrase passed her lips as she stared at the beautiful woman.

"Hello, I'm Allana, leader of the Tuscola Clan." She held her hand out to Cade and he took it. Unlike Jacqui, he'd shaken off his initial reaction and gone back to normal. He smiled as he looked at his wife's stunned face.

"Allana, this is my wife, Jacqui, and I'm Cade of the Alexander Clan."

"It seems we have some work to do." Allana looked at the pile of 13 people on the floor of the main room as her people came into the room. "If your wife could release them…?"

Jacqui shook herself from her stupor and looked over at the men and women on the floor. She'd seen bruises on Damesha's face and Cade knew what she was thinking. She wanted to make them all pay whether they had anything to do with Damesha's pain and bruises or not.

"Later, princess. Let Allana handle this. This is her territory. We must not intrude more than we already have." Cade spoke to her gently, taking her in his arms.

"If I must." Jacqui let out a long slow exhalation, and

the people on the floor started to move as Allana's people took them away.

"I'll need one of your representatives to come, a statement from you both and from your brother and his wife, but you can go now. I have my people at the hotel where your brother is. You'll be safe. But I think you are already. Your wife is… special, isn't she?" Allana's blue eyes searched over Jacqui, a curiosity there that made Cade prickle a little. Jacqui was his.

"Yes, she is. There aren't many like her left." Cade spoke the truth, witches were rare now and Jacqui was very special. She was his wife, not just a witch. He took her under his arm and they left, heading to the hotel in Houma.

12

Jacqui

"This is all very messy isn't it?" Jacqui asked as they settled into their bed later that night, Mary at their feet.

"It is but we'll sort it tomorrow. At least Mary's letting us know when she needs to go out. For now, I just want to hold you. That was utterly astonishing and I knew you would be safe with me, but damn Jacqui. You kicked ass!" Cade was impressed now that a shower and some more food had helped it to all sink in.

"I'm pretty impressed with myself. Something just snapped in my head and I knew what I needed to do. Evelyn warned me this could happen. I didn't really believe her, but wow." They snuggled together under the covers, and Jacqui's hands began to wander.

"I didn't plan on loving you. I was just looking for a wife to shut people up, but I'm so glad I chose you." Cade pulled her up over him, her legs straddling his hips as she looked down at him.

"I didn't plan on loving you either. I planned a nice boring life, with no excitement, no worries and no love. I was afraid to love, terrified of it. But it started with Damesha. Then you. And Elspeth and Annie and now, sometimes I feel like I'm going to explode from all of the love I feel. You gave me that, Cade, you melted the walls with that first email we shared. I had no idea you were doing it but you and your family, well, you've changed my life for the better." She leaned over to listen to his strong heart beating in his chest, the most reassuring sound in the world.

Cade stroked her back, staring up at the ceiling as he inhaled the clean scent of her hair.

"I know it makes us weak but that's part of the thrill of love, isn't it? Giving up part of your control, part of your security, to share in another person's life. I was terrified of falling into the same trap my parents fell into, of leaving behind a child that would have to experience what I went through. But we can change that, can't we? Together, with the help of the other clans, we can end this threat once and for all. I know we can." He pressed up into her, his mind already on the delights hidden between her thighs.

He pushed her up gently, cupping her breasts. "They're heavier."

"Yes, which is another reason we have to end this now. Anastasia cannot grow up in this world the Mungons have planned. We have to stop them." She pressed down into his hard length, moving gently to entice him with her wet heat. His fingers on her breasts created an ache inside of her that she needed filled.

"We'll do it together, princess. That's the only way it can be done." Cade rolled her to her back, entering her expertly as he did so.

They cried out together as they lost themselves to the passion that only the other could stir. This had not been the plan at all, love was the last thing they'd wanted. But love had found them and they would, had to, fight to maintain it. Life wasn't going to be the simple plan that Jacqui had in mind, or the chaotic but ordered plan Cade had wanted. But it was worth fighting for now and fight they would, to their dying breaths if need be.

DELETED SCENES

Cade

Islid between my wife and the Alpha of the clan we'd allied with. Allana was beautiful, seductive, and fuckably tempting. I watched her as she stared into my wife's icy eyes, eyes that now seemed warm instead of cold. Jacqui was interested in Allana, I could see it in the way her tongue darted out to wet her bottom lip, and the way her eyes would go wide when she caught the woman's scent.

I didn't mind if my wife had a fascination with another woman, what man wouldn't get hard just considering it? No, I didn't mind it, but I wondered where I fit into it all. Allana was far too interested, I wasn't too blinded by my wife's beauty to recognize that. Shifters are forward by nature at times, especially when they want something, but in most cases we are reserved around non-shifters. Even as my wife, especially as my wife, Allana should not be so open with Jacqui. Something wasn't right.

The redhead with the swirling green eyes turned her gaze to me, offering an invitation I wasn't sure I should take for two reasons. The first one was my discomfort at her performance, I wasn't one to turn away from a sultry gaze but something wasn't right here. The second was my very pregnant wife.

"Honey, I think we should head to bed. You're tired." I took her arm, sitting up from my stool at the bar in the former monastery we were using as a refuge.

She snuggled up to me, her gaze flitting to Allana to give her a wink before turning back to me.

"Mm, that sounds like a very good idea. Shall we bring Allana with us?" Their gazes caught once more, desire a surging invisible wave between them.

I considered it for a moment, my heart pounding and my dick turning into a rock as images coursed through my brain. The two of them together would be a sight to behold, their pale skin tangled together, blond hair mixing with red as they writhed. Fuck, I can't breathe!

"Uh, do you think that's a good idea?" I whispered it into her ear, the urge to tease her with my lips, just below her ear, too strong to fight. She shivered in my arms, her taut belly pressing into me. She'd been so fucking horny since becoming pregnant, even her increasing size doing little to flatten her need. I glanced at Allana from over Jacqui's head, her eyes begging for just a moment with us.

How could I turn that down?

Allana came behind Jacqui, her arms going around my wife's waist to cup her full breasts. My eyes glued to those pale fingers teasing at Jacqui's nipples through her shirt. Jacqui moaned quietly, her head going back on Allana's shoulder. She wanted Allana.

I wanted to give her to Jacqui, I so wanted to let her have what she wanted the most at this moment.

My will crumbled as Allana's fingers gripped more tightly at my wife's nipples, making her moan louder and her knees wobbled. I caught my wife staring into Allana's eyes. There was challenge there, a dare that I didn't want to turn down. I reached out, touching her silky cheek, my thumb tracing down her cheek to her full lips.

I'd love to see those lips wrapped around Jacqui's clit, or her nipples. Or my dick.

"Please, baby. Just this one time." Jacqui's words came out on a shiver, her need making her plead.

Jacqui's hand went between us, cupping my rigid length through the tight jeans I wore. The bar was dimly lit, and we were the only patrons in sight so I didn't care about anyone watching. When Jacqui squeezed me gently, insistently, and purred against the pulse in my throat, my will disappeared.

I took her lips with mine, my skin already heated and aching for her touch. I did love my wife, after all, and her eager need for sex always inflamed me. Not bad for a woman that came to me as an untouched virgin.

I grasped the top of her arms with both hands, holding her to me as our tongues twined together slickly. Allana's hands pressed between us, on Jacqui's breasts, kneading gently at the tender globes. Oh, how could I say no to this, this erotic entanglement that could spell disaster for us all.

I pulled away from Jacqui's seeking tongue, looking down into her eyes.

The fire in her eyes shocked me, shook me, and I knew I couldn't tell her no. Allana was up to something, I knew that, but Jacqui didn't care, she only wanted the woman with a passion that drove her insatiably.

"Alright." I couldn't say anything more because Jacqui

pulled my head down to hers once more, her lips fusing to mine with her relief.

I felt Allana's hand, so different from my wife's touch, playing along our lips, and Jacqui pulled away, taking a finger into her moist heat. I watched, entranced as the finger disappeared between my wife's lips, the image doing its job well. I grew impossibly hard.

"Let's go." I took my wife's hand, my only thought on getting us all to our bedroom before we lost all sense.

We were barely out of the bar before I saw my brother, Jacob heading towards me, his face an unreadable mask. At the same time, a chirping noise came from Allana's direction and I saw her stiffen. She took out a phone and walked a short distance away.

I watched her as Jacob approached us, still feeling a tingle of doubt in the back of my mind. Jacqui shifted impatiently beside me, her need making her all but dance. I soothed her hair down her back, kissing the top of her head.

"It's alright, darling, you know I'll take care of you." Jacob reached us and I turned to face him. "What's up, brother?"

"It's Jadrian." His face, so similar to my own, was now a map of anger. I knew this wasn't going to be good. "He's out. Hunting."

I swore as Jacob finished, my hand digging through my hair in frustration. I didn't need this right now!

"Find him. Watch him!" Jacob nodded in acknowledgment, his eyes looking straight into mine. "Don't stop him, but keep him out of trouble. We have a very important meeting in a few hours. He can't miss it. Do you understand?"

"I do, Cade. He'll be here, one way or another." Jacob didn't say anything more, he just turned and left, knowing I had little more to add.

I turned around to my wife, her mewl of distress catching my attention. Allana was stalking off down the other end of the hall, heading in the wrong direction. I guess one of her own people needed her. She'd been like a cat in heat and now she left without an explanation. There was a lot going on right now, and I wasn't the only one with responsibilities.

"Next time, baby." The fact that Jadrian was out hunting vampire blood had dulled the edge of my desire but my wife was miserable, she needed release, and right now that was the most important duty I had. "Come on, let me take care of you."

She grinned, and I felt relief that she didn't complain. I was enough for her. Yeah, a bit old-fashioned but for a moment I'd wondered if I'd be able to handle her if I'd refused her plea. I knew now she just wanted the experience, that she would always come back to me and do it gladly.

"Make me purr, darling." She begged as we made our way into our bedroom, more a chamber than a room. A large bed filled the room and someone already had the fire going. The rooms here were always cold, even in the heat of summer.

I left the lights off, letting the fire guide us, and picked my wife up. Sitting down with her in my lap I began to kiss her as she undid the buttons of her blouse, baring herself to me. Her breasts were full, tight, and ready for my touch.

Tight nipples begged for hot lips and I answered their plea.

With a gasp she pressed the hot flesh further into my mouth, her fingers grasping at my hair to hold me in place as my tongue teased the puckered flesh. I felt her grind in my lap, her round ass pressing into my engorged cock.

"Oh, Jacqui, I won't last long if you keep that up." I gasped against her skin as she continued her lap dance, teasing me.

I pushed the length of her long pale green skirt away from her thighs, seeking out her damp folds. Her heavy breathing told me she only needed a little bit of a push and she'd explode in my arms, and I wanted to give her the release.

I found her wet and ready for my entry, my fingers sliding into her easily, without touching the most important rigid button yet. My wife, slim and fragile when she wasn't pregnant, was now heavier and rounder with her pregnancy, but I held her easily as she began to grind faster, fucking my fingers without any aid from me at all.

She was so fucking ready! I sucked at her nipple harder, my tongue laving over the sensitive skin, as she began to quiver in my arms. Her walls, tight and hot, pulsed around my fingers and I knew she was coming.

She gasped as her body shook around me, making me ache to be inside of her, to spill myself in her heated confines, but I held back, letting her have this first orgasm unhindered, to take the edge off.

As she came down, her panting gasps of breath finally turning to even breathing, I fell back on the bed. She climbed over me, her skirt gone now, and started to pull my shirt open but left it on as she slid down my body, her fingers playing over my own nipples for a moment before trailing down to where her tongue traced circles just above the button of my jeans.

"You were very good tonight, Cade." Her breathless voice came to me, thrilling my ears just as her fingers undid the button, letting it pop free.

I was so hard, so ready, that my cock pushed down the zipper and her fingers wrapped around me. I shifted just enough to push my pants away, Jacqui helping to slide them off completely but she didn't let go of my cock.

"I so wanted to bring Allana back here so I could watch her suck your cock, Cade." Her tongue lashed out with each word, swirling, darting, tasting me.

Her words painted a picture in my head, her tongue filled in the rest.

"Fuck, Jacqui, baby, you're so good!" I plunged a hand into her hair, holding her head for a moment as I fucked her mouth, her lips sliding down my shaft before the head popped free, only to plunge back in.

I was going to get off too fast, so I pulled out, letting her grip me with her hand as she looked up at me with eyes slightly darker than their normal almost translucent color.

"I have to fuck you now, Cade. I can't wait." She crawled up my strong body, straddling my hips. She hovered over me, her grip tracing my cock along her slick folds. She looked lost in her own world.

"Did you want to watch her fucking me, Jacqui? Did you want to sit on my face, letting my tongue fuck that sweet pussy of yours while you kissed her?" She opened her eyes, her witchy eyes, a light seeming to glow within them now. "Did you want to tease her nipples as she rode up and down my cock, is that what you wanted, baby?"

My own words were having an effect on me and if she didn't slide down my cock soon I was going to plunge it straight up into her. I moved my hands down to the place where her legs met her body, pushing gently. She smiled then, a sexy devilish smile that made my toes curl.

"All of that and more, Cade. I wanted to lick her pussy until she screamed my name, while you fucked me, staring down at us both. Oh yes, I wanted to get my hands on those gorgeous breasts of hers, and my fingers in her pussy while you watched, I wanted so many different," she paused then and I felt her pussy splitting open as she slid down onto my cock, "things."

I supported her as we gasped together, watching as she sat back, finding just the right angle as she began a grinding motion that soon had her gasping out moans of pleasure.

I reached between us, sliding my fingers into her wet heat until I found her clit and began a clockwise circle with just the right pressure. I felt her clench around me, her hands going up to clutch at her full breasts, plucking at her nipples as words began to stream out of her mouth.

I waited, watching, wanting her to have her fill, gritting my teeth against the urge to come. She was so fucking wet, so incredibly hot, scorching hot around my dick, and I wanted nothing more than to lose myself in her, but she had to come again first.

"Cade, oh baby, it would have been so good. Please, promise me, we're going to have that, please." She writhed her hips, an expert at riding my dick now, and I felt the first shock of her orgasm as she clenched around my dick.

I took in a deep breath, preparing for what was coming. I held her hips but didn't stop her as she began to writhe faster, her motions more than I could resist now. I let myself go, following with her as she rode me into bliss.

I could feel the first surge as my balls shot my load up into her, and the answering response as her walls milked me from the inside. Incredible.

We moved together, in tune with one another, lost in each other, until the surging and pulsing stopped. She came down to rest beside me and we clung together, my lips going out to kiss her damp forehead.

"I love you, Jacqui."

"Not as much as I love you, Cade. Thank you, baby." I wasn't sure why she was thanking me but I was too busy drifting into sleep to ask.

We'd both need our rest for what was coming. A battle like no other, and then our baby. Life was never guaranteed and for now, I was going to take these moments with her, and any other moments, that might come our way. We might not have another chance if we lose this coming war.

ABOUT THE AUTHOR

Selina Coffey is a romance writer who lives happily in London with her husband and son. She is a hopeless romantic who grew up always believing in love and she is not ashamed to admit this! It is this belief that makes her so passionate about writing crazy love stories.

A stereotypical girly girl, she loves shopping. So whenever she gets a chance and the spare cash, you will probably find her browsing online for the next pair of shoes to add to her collection.!

You can find her online at
www.selinacoffey.com

Contact her at
hello@selinacoffey.com